MAVERICK HEART

by

Rebecca Marsh

Author of "THE WALKS OF DREAMS," "TIGER IN HER HEART" *and* "LADY DETECTIVE"

Publicist Opal Bondy had cheerfully undertaken many difficult assignments for her employer Mike Lane. But she balked at the assignment to transform a cattle baron's range-wild daughter, Maverick Prather, into a gracious lady worthy of marriage to Tate Craithorne. In the first place, Opal's instincts told her that riding herd on Maverick would be physically dangerous. And in the second place, gossip told Opal that professional failure would cost her both Mike and her job.

Faced with this challenge, Opal decided to fight fire with fire by becoming a maverick herself. But in the process of trying to frighten Maverick into submission and to outthink Mike Lane, Opal made the shattering discovery that she, too, had a maverick heart that would be satisfied with nothing less than the love it really wanted.

MAVERICK HEART

Maverick Heart

by

REBECCA MARSH

By

Sharon Publications Inc.
Cresskill, N.J.

Fourth Printing 1983

Copyright © MCMLXI by Arcadia House
Published by
Sharon Publications Inc.
Cresskill, N.J.

Printed in the U.S.A.
Cover illustrations by Joan Croom
ISBN 0-89531-134-8

MAVERICK HEART

Chapter 1

In Tincup, Texas, on the morning of April tenth, a burly oil baron kicked at a dog on the corner of First Street and Grove Avenue. The first kick missed, but not the second; a fact the oil baron noted ruefully was depicted in a front-page photograph in the *Texas Informer*. He laid the proof on Opal Bondy's desk. He wagged his bald, sun-raddled head. He asked: "You know what they should do to photographers in this country?"

"Why did you kick the dog, sir?"

"What they should do is smash their cameras and give them polecats a hemp necktie!"

"Have you told the newspaper that?"

"Some other things, too. Nobody gets away

with making Jeb Agnew look bad."

Opal got the *Texas Informer* on the telephone. Sally was warmly friendly until Opal stated her hope the newspaper would overlook Mr. Agnew's intemperate words. Then Sally got tough. "Listen, honey," she said, "your company can't do a thing for that cayuse. I wouldn't have the nerve to tell my boss you want us to give him a break. You know what happened to that dog?"

"What?"

"The kick broke a rib, the rib punctured a lung, the dog had to be shot."

Opal swallowed.

"Then on top of that, honey, this cayuse comes here and actually threatens to punch my boss if he doesn't fire the photographer, kill the story and apologize publicly for printing that picture."

"On the other hand, though—"

"Anything else," Sally interrupted, "that we can do for the Lane Public Relations Company?"

Opal pronged the handset. She ignored the hard blue eyes stabbing at her face. Instinct told her to be careful, very careful, but she found it difficult to control her tongue. "The dog had to be shot," she told the oil baron. "Your kick broke a rib, the rib punctured a lung. Your threat to punch the editor of the paper unless he did certain things hasn't helped matters, of course."

All that was brushed aside with a violent sweep of his hand. "If I didn't need help I wouldn't be here. Take care of it today, Miss Bondy. If they don't kill the story, the Agnew Oil Exploration Company will find somebody else to handle its publicity."

He jumped up, grabbed his Stetson from the costumer, and went out swiftly. A minute or two later, Opal saw him gun his purple Cadillac convertible up the street with startling indifference to the speed law. He just missed a woman in the crosswalk. His left-hand turn into Jenkins Way was accompanied by tire squeals she could hear half a block away. Some day, she thought moodily, he'd kill or maim someone with his car, and neither Mike nor herself nor any other publicist would be able to do a thing for him even if he wanted to.

She gave the problem thought, revolted by its details but interested professionally in the challenge it offered her ability. It was at once obvious to her that some darned good explanation of the dog kicking would have to be prepared in a hurry. Texans didn't cotton to folks who were brutal to animals, period. Then something else would have to be prepared to counter the effects of the story the *Texas Informer* was certain to print on the subject of Mr. Agnew's threats. And finally, Mr. Agnew or his company would have to hit the headlines so favorably people would be maneuvered into thinking this self-made man was a pretty darned fine character after all.

Opal went to work. She summarized the problem to clarify it for herself as well as for Mike Lane. She then outlined the three-phase method she thought could be used to solve the problem. Under the dog-kicking heading, she sketched the outlines of four explanations which she thought reasonable people would accept in extenuation of the seeming brutality. But she could get no further then, because Kitty stepped in to announce the arrival of Mrs. Wentworth herself. Kitty was beside herself with excitement. "Miss Bondy," she said, "she's just as beautiful now as when she was a motion picture star. I recognized her the instant she stepped in. You know that red hair of hers? Well, it's her own, all right, and it's genuine red."

"Mike?"

Kitty rolled her big gray eyes. "Up the street having coffee with the boys, Miss Bondy. I kept telling him Mrs. Wentworth was scheduled for ten, but he didn't pay any attention."

Opal barely repressed a grin. "Probably he heard you," she said, "but wished he hadn't. Women tend to scare Mike; isn't that strange?"

"I know a lot of women in Tincup who'd like to show him there's nothing to fear!"

"But I saw him first, Kitty, remember?"

Kitty was quite indignant. "Miss Bondy, would I do a thing like that to you? Why, the very idea! I'm just not that sort of woman."

Opal continued to think otherwise, but she said she was very glad to know she could cross one rival off her list and told Kitty to send Mrs. Wentworth to her in five minutes. She utilized the time to freshen up in the lavatory and to study the letter Mrs. Wentworth had written to brief Mike on reasons for wanting an appointment. When Mrs. Wentworth stepped in, Opal was deliberately standing at one of the windows, the letter in her hand but her eyes engrossed in a study of the street scene. She forced Mrs. Wentworth to clear her throat for attention. She turned then, quite casually, and said: "Oh, you must be Mrs. Wentworth. I think I would recognize you anywhere. Do sit down, won't you? Mr. Lane was called out on pressing business, and rather than have you wait for him, I thought I could dispose of the preliminaries."

Mrs. Wentworth sat down in the leather armchair facing the desk. Her face, piquant in its thinness and bone structure, took on a dubious expression. "Aren't you rather young for this?" she asked. "I particularly require a publicist of vast experience."

"I like to imagine, Mrs. Wentworth, that my

genius counts for more than vast routine experience. I know that's for you to judge, however; and in any event, Mr. Lane will direct whatever affairs you entrust to us."

Now the famous green eyes began to twinkle. "That was quick," Mrs. Wentworth complimented her. "Put you in the Hollywood rat race a year or two, and you'd be quicker than most. What experience have you had?"

"College education and training, and on-the-job training in New York City and here."

"Texas girl?"

"Very much so."

"Ranch girl?"

"City girl. San Antonio, in fact."

"Well, that's to your credit. I haven't much use for ranch people. I don't think you grow appreciably or learn much if you spend most of your time with cattle and horses. I find them very uninspiring, myself."

Opal took her chair and made herself quite comfortable. She found it nerve-wracking to remain cool and businesslike in the presence of one of her motion picture idols. As Kitty had said, the hair was her own and the color was genuine.

Mrs. Wentworth removed her lightweight beige coat and got down to busines. "What I'm seeking," she said, "is what you might call career insurance. I'm really quite happy in my marriage to Mr. Wentworth. While it is true that he is somewhat older and more sedentary than I, we have much in common, not the least of which are enthusiasm for the arts, a pasison for travel and a strong interest in business matters. So you mustn't misunderstand my concern for my career. But one does have to be practical, you know, particularly when one is known as a four or five-million-dollar piece of property. If for one reason or another I had to resume my career, I would want to resume it as at least a million-dollar piece of property."

"Quite understandable, Mrs. Wentworth. I may as well confess those figures you've mentioned are rather startling to me."

"One of the reasons I wondered about your professional experience and competence. I mean no offense when I say this building, this office, your clothes, are not of the quality that inspires respect for your business accomplishments."

Opal recalled in the nick of time that the woman had approached them despite the visible shabbiness of the one-story building that housed the company. The recollection enabled her to endure stoically the woman's opinion of her home-made suit.

"Precisely what did you think we could do for you, Mrs. Worthington?" she fenced. "Possibly we're not qualified to handle anything for you. If that is the case, I'll tell you so frankly."

"A regular campaign designed to keep my name before the public. Little human interest stories released at regular intervals to the press. Little anecdotes concerning my life here for distribution to professional organs and clubs and other societies. My primary concern is that I not be forgotten. Of course I will make a motion picture or so a year and perhaps appear in television occasionally simply to keep my face and my name in the public eye. Those appearances, in addition to regular publicity, ought to serve my purpose, I think."

Opal jotted it down in shorthand, studied it, then smiled with a confidence she certainly didn't feel. "Nothing difficult in any of this, Mrs. Wentworth, inasmuch as the major publicity involving your appearances would be handled by a major house with connections everywhere. This is a little local stuff, it seems to me, and nothing more."

"I could be persuaded to give you a try. If you deliver the goods, I could enter into a formal contract for your services."

"We'd do our best, Mrs. Wentworth. That goes without saying. Suppose I brief Mr. Lane for you? I'm sure he'd be happy to draw up some plans for you to consider."

"On the other hand, Miss Bondy, I might have an idea right this minute that I want you to execute for me. I thought that if I were to go to the sheriff and demand that Mr. Jeb Agnew be arrested for murdering a dog—"

She broke off, amused by Opal's expression. "A prior commitment to Mr. Agnew?" she asked.

"I think so, Mrs. Wentworth. And I don't imagine you'd believe me if I were to tell you the publicity you could derive from having him arrested wouldn't be worth the effort."

"I don't think I'd believe you, Miss Bondy. But why not discuss the whole matter with Mr. Lane? He may call me at any time before three o'clock this afternoon."

Mrs. Wentworth rose gracefully and Opal helped her with her coat. She had Kitty escort the woman to her car, and after Kitty returned she herself walked up the block to break up Mike's morning conference with the "boys" in the first booth in Cal's Good Eats. Mike wasn't happy to see her. "Bother me later," he snapped; "you're interrupting an argument." But he came outdoors quickly enough after she'd told him it was something of an emergency. As she recounted events he listened attentively and his quick, realistic mind separated the wheat from the chaff. He dismissed Mr. Agnew's threats to manhandle the editor of the *Texas Informer* as hot-headed chatter easily stopped by an apology. On the other hand, he accepted as a grave problem the fact that the dog had had to be shot. "Tough to cope with," he said at that point. The Wentworth matter, conversely, was taken very seriously from beginning to end. "An assignment such as that could make us nationally," he snapped. "The best thing would be to grab her and toss out Agnew. Only trouble there, however, is that Agnew gives us an annual retainer plus fees and our deal is a long-term deal. I'll work on Mrs. Wentworth. Eliminate her interest in using the dog for a publicity gimmick, and we could do business here and now. You go to work on Agnew and leave the rest to me."

"My conscience will trouble me, you know. He's a thoroughly unpleasant man."

"But will it trouble you to marry the rich president of an important public relations firm?"

"Then you're seriously considering giving me that promotion?"

His black eyes danced. Then quickly, before she could move, Mike Lane pulled her close and kissed her.

Chapter 2

Editor Bert Nutting of the *Texas Informer* was a big man in his late thirties, a man esteemed in Tincup as much for his combat record in two wars as for his knowledge of the town and his profession. He stood up and gave Opal a firm handshake. "Always a pleasure," he said, and it was clear that he meant it. Yet his first words after she'd gotten seated made it equally clear he was not killing any story to please her or anyone else. "I've told Sally to get you a proof of the Agnew yarn we're printing this afternoon. I wanted to write it myself, but doubted I could be objective. I like an objective writer."

"Full bombardment, Bert?"

"With all the howitzers in my arsenal. And I know the size of the man and the ferocity of his temperament, so don't remind me of those."

"Yet I'm ordered to get him off the hook, Bert. Wretched problem to be given on a Friday morning. I'll probably spend the whole weekend stewing."

"And you should!" he said ringingly. "I say that under Mike Lane you're learning to cut too many corners. Now you listen to a fellow who likes you. A buck is a buck, and we can't survive without our fair share of 'em. But some things may be done for a buck and other things ought not to be done. Puffery is legitimate up to a certain point only."

"On the other hand, Bert, we are in business to help people create a favorable attitude toward them and their products. If we examined the motives of every person who sought our help, we'd starve to death. And it's the same here, don't ever think otherwise. Every day you print advertisements so untruthful it's a disgrace."

"Not knowingly."

"But you print them. That's the big thing. And the only reason you don't know this claim is true and this claim is false is that you don't take the trouble to investigate them. That brings us to Mr. Agnew. Right now I don't know all the circumstances of the case. I assume he had a perfectly good reason for kicking that dog. I don't say that I would kick a dog under any circumstances, but I do say he's entitled to the benefit of the doubt until someone can investigate the matter."

His eyes, golden brown, snapped to attention and saluted her. "Very, very clever," he said. "You came here, I gather, not to ask me to kill the story but to sit on it while you investigate?"

"Yup."

He loved her twinkling blue eyes in that moment. He slapped the desk forcefully. "Okay," he boomed, "let's get to City Hall and get our marriage over with. You've just won me. A girl that clever has to be my wife."

"Will you sit on the story, Bert?"

He gave it thought, his beefy face solemn. "I suppose if I don't, it'll hurt you?"

"Not personally, to be honest. But profession-ally, yes."

"In that case, no. I couldn't care less about your career. When you came back from New York two years ago, you were a credit to Tincup and to Texas. But under this Lane fellow, this sharp-shooter, this double-crosser, this chaser after women, this—"

"Stop it!"

Bert stopped it. Her face was genuinely angry, and he was too intelligent to prod her further.

"If you won't do it to help me, Bert, consider this: Mr. Agnew will sue for every penny your publisher has. He will sue for libel, defamation of character and gross damage to his business inter-ests."

"He'd have to prove his case."

"No. You make statements in that story, so it will be up to you to prove your case."

Sally brought in the galley of the second Ag-new story. "Still wet," she said; "better not han-dle it." She laid the galley on the desk and looked curiously at Opal's pale blue suit. "Nice suit," she said a bit wistfully. "Make it, honey?"

"Well, Mom did do a few things, such as cutting and basting and stitching and fitting. And stop looking so envious. You've been told before and I'll tell you again: the sewing room at our place can always accommodate one more seamstress."

"The trouble is that I'm lazy. I do want the clothes; what woman doesn't? But I just can't seem to generate the old energy."

"Read!" Bert ordered. "I'm a busy man!"

Opal read, and was soon wincing. It was at once clear that Bert had written the story even though someone else had been given the byline. The piece was Bert at his most trenchant, a brilliant piece that stripped Jeb Agnew of the strength of his youth, his intelligence, his common sense, his fabulous energy and perception to reveal him for the man he now was: a violent and bombastic man, a rather foolish oldster who had deluded himself into believing that the legend his public relations experts had created for him was fact and not fantasy.

The highlight of the story, the "threat scene" itself, was devastating savagery. You saw the bald, bellowing old man hopping up and down with fury and looking perfectly ridiculous as he threatened to punch two hundred pounds of hard-jawed, hard-fisted, combat-trained youth into submission. And then, to cap the climax, you saw none other than Sally grab the old man by the ear and march him off as a mother might march off her howling little son. . . .

The professional writer in Opal was stirred. "I wish I could write like that," she said. "Then I'd be a writer and not a publicist's flunky. Very, very good."

"Think nothing of it," Bert said. "The fellow who wrote it happens to be a genius."

He waved Sally from the office and they went back to their discussion. "About proving our case, Opal," Bert went on: "We have the photograph and witnesses to prove he kicked the dog. We have witnesses here to prove he really did threaten me. I don't think suing us will accomplish anything but make Agnew look more ridiculous."

"Still—"

"One thing more. You may hate me for this, but I'll risk it. Mike knew darned well he himself didn't have a chance to get us to kill this story. So he sent you, knowing that I like you, knowing that I usually end up doing what you ask. Well, I resent that. And I resent it when a girl who should know better allows herself to be used this way."

"Still—"

An incredible thing happened. Big Bert stood up and took a long step toward the office door. "I've said all I will say on the subject, Opal. The story hits the stands this afternoon."

"Give me until tomorrow, please. Is that asking too much? I just have to ask Mr. Agnew a few questions."

But it fell on deaf ears. Bert walked out, and presently Sally stepped in unhappily to announce that the interview was over.

It shook Opal. "Hey," she protested, "what have I done to deserve such treatment? Where's that good old professional courtesy Bert talks of?"

"I wouldn't know, honey. I guess Bert's tired of helping Mike Lane by giving you all the breaks he can. What about all the Bondys for chow tomorrow night at my place? Real barbecue."

"Great. I'll bring the salad, though."

Sally hesitated and then asked: "Do you have to stick to Agnew? Girl to girl, honey, a client like that would make me feel pretty uneasy."

"We've accepted his retainers for three years. You can hardly dump a client, can you, the moment he becomes a problem?"

Sally said she didn't see why not, and Opal was in too much of a hurry to treat her to a lecture on the ethics of the publicist's profession. Opal went back to her Ford station wagon, gave her next step some thought, then drove on up Central Street to the great four-story, pseudo adobe-brick building that housed police headquarters and the jail. A police lieutenant was detailed by the Chief himself to provide her with all the information they had on the dog-kicking episode, and the lieutenant led her along a freshly painted hall to the records room. He found the information she wanted and stood wagging his head while she scribbled down the essential facts in shorthand. "If it was me," he commented, "I'd have shot that dog. I guess the only reason Agnew didn't is he was afraid a bullet would go wild. How's his leg?"

"Leg?"

"Dog slashed at him. One of the boys who went out on the call gave him some first-aid and told him to go see a doctor. Dog didn't have rabies, though. I guess that poor hound dog was pretty hungry and thirsty and scared right there in the busiest section of town. I guess it was just Agnew's luck to be there when the dog sort of blew his top."

"You mean that Mr. Agnew was actually bitten?"

"More slashed than bitten, Miss Bondy."

It puzzled Opal. "Was the reporter told?"

"What reporter? Wasn't a reporter there. Somebody took a picture, I know, because I saw it in the *Informer*. But there wasn't a reporter around when we got there."

"But it is a matter of record, Lieutenant, that Mr. Agnew was either slashed or bitten by that animal before he kicked it in self-defense?"

The lieutenant riffled through the report on the episode and finally pointed to a paragraph. Opal copied the paragraph exactly. She then asked if she could have a photostatic copy of the full report, and that request brought her face to face with the Chief once more.

"What's up?" the Chief asked bluntly. "Our records are public records, always available when authorized persons want to see them. I know the outfit you work for, Miss Bondy. Mike Lane spearheaded a drive last year to collect money for the wife of one of our men who was killed in the line of duty. In our book, you're a good outfit, so we're on your side. But being policemen, we have to be totally neutral when something involving a case we've handled comes up."

"Well," she countered, grinning, "will you telephone Bert Nutting of the *Informer* and give him the information covering the self-defense angle? Tell him it's my way of thanking him for past kindnesses. And will you tell him, also, I'll enjoy reading his revised story on the incident in this afternoon's paper? Tell him it's urgent that the revised story be printed this afternoon."

He scratched his head.

"Ah," she said, "he won't speak to me right now, Chief. Weren't you ever young and foolish?"

He laughed and said he'd oblige her, and Opal drove on through the warm morning to Mr. Agnew's great home on the fringe of the ranch country. A maid answered the door and smiled in friendly fashion and led her through another door at the end of the main hall into a large, flagstoned patio. Mr. Agnew was sitting in a canvas butterfly chair before a large rectangular fish pond. He was tossing crumbs into the pool and chattering away in husky tones to the fish rising to eat. He wasn't at all pleased to be interrupted, but he was polite enough to wave her to a chair and tell her she could have five minutes.

"Mission accomplished," Opal told him. "The *Informer* will print a revised version of the story this afternoon."

"What changed their mind?"

"May I ask a question, sir?"

"No. You're paid to answer questions, and Jeb Agnew gets what he pays for."

"You pay Mr. Lane," Opal said, "not me. The question I want to ask is this: why didn't you tell Mr. Nutting that the dog had slashed your leg first, that you kicked in self-defense?"

A frozen expression came onto his face. "Who told you that?"

"Public record at police headquarters, sir. Incidentally, a check revealed the dog didn't have rabies."

"Who told you to go to police headquarters?"

"No one. You do what you can to prevent unfavorable stories from being printed about your client. I think Mr. Nutting will cancel the very brilliant story he wrote about that scene you made in his office."

Jeb Agnew drew a deep breath. "If I'd wanted

the slashing made public, I'd have made it public."

Opal looked at her watch and rose. "There's my report, sir."

"Nobody bites me and gets away with it," he snapped. "No hound dog, no two-bit editor. I wanted to hit him with that self-defense thing when it would hurt. Now I can't. I don't like that."

"That's what I thought," Opal said. "That's why I gave Bert Nutting the full information."

As his face turned purple-red, Opal smiled and nodded and left.

Chapter 3

At Sally Raine's barbecue the following evening, Bert Nutting said thanks and then said more. "Opal," he said, "let me find you a real job. A girl so quick on her mental feet is wasted at Lane's. Care to work for Bruce Prather?"

"Nope."

"Big man, Prather. Probably the biggest rancher in this corner of Texas. They say that if all the stock he owns were driven past the same point, the drive would take a full day and the earth would tremble. A man that big might pay you a dollar an hour."

"What would I do with such vast wealth, Bert? A girl doesn't work for money alone."

Sally came over, very striking in riding pants and clean wool shirt and pink embroidered organdie apron. "Like?" Sally asked Opal. "This idiot thought that a girl giving a barbecue might need an apron. Didn't the salesgirl see him coming, though!"

"Or maybe," Bert chuckled, "I saw the salesgirl before she saw me."

Sally aimed a mock clout at his chin, but she was such a short dumpling and he was such a towering oaf her tiny fist missed by at least eighteen inches. "Anyway," she said, "I love this apron, duded up though I feel."

Others came along at last, Opal's mother and father among them. Sally led Bert off to light all the kerosene torches, overcoming his protests with the statement the sun would set sooner or later and they might as well get that chore out of the way. Opal got the huge bucket of salad from her father and went over to the work and serving tables near the barbecue pit. The work gang, she discovered, was under the supervision of Sally's grandmother, and Mrs. Benson wasn't one to per-

mit just any old chow to be served her granddaughter's guests. She gave the bucket a dubious
glance. "You think you're feedin' hogs or some-
thin'?" she asked. "What you got in that bucket,
Opal?"

"Greens of all kinds. I have the dressing to
work in if you have some bowls I can use."

First the bucket had to be opened and the
crispness and taste of the greens tested. Only then
did Mrs. Benson fetch some bowls and tools to
work with, and she made it quite clear that she
disapproved of such fare. "Folks don't go much
for greens," she opined. "Fill 'em with meat and
drink; that satisfies 'em."

But the arrival of other guests sent her scurry-
ing to the gate, and a couple of younger and less
dubious women came over, grinning, to lend a
hand. Pretty soon the salad mixing was going
well, and the gossip, too.

"Opal," Mrs. Tinston asked, "guess what
about Maverick Prather?"

"What?"

"Can't you guess?"

"She told Preacher Stone he'd yell a better sermon with some rum in him."

Mrs. Pilger said loftily: "Kid stuff; try again."

"She lost a million or so playing poker."

"They say," Mrs. Tinston then announced dramatically, "that Maverick and her Pa are squabbling about Tate Craithorne. He's all for her marrying Tate yesterday, but she's all for marrying Tate next year or something."

It was odd, Opal thought, how in almost every community there was one family so big, so much in the public eye and mind, that its every affair was discussed at length and made much of by most of the other folks in town.

"You think it would be a good idea?" Mrs. Tinston asked. "Personally, I don't hold with girls marrying before they know what life is about. Here's what I mean. Just take a look around at all those roosters waiting for their chuck! See them strutting around and crowing? You might get the notion, if you didn't know what life is about, that those roosters have real brains and real strength. But that isn't so. Take the wives out of their homes, out of this community, and you'd see those roosters running around in circles, just like roosters with their heads chopped off. It's us women who put order and sense into life, and how can a girl do that for her husband if she don't know what life is all about?"

Mrs. Pilger nodded in excited agreement. She was reminded of a true story, she said, and she proceeded to narrate the story while the sun dropped below the horizon and all the clouds and land turned red and purple.

"Now this family," Mrs. Pilger said, "was quite challenging to a social worker. There was no reason for it to be supported by the county. The father was an able-bodied, thoroughly competent carpenter. The mother was intelligent, industrious, thrifty. The boy, about fifteen, was a quick and personable lad who did odd jobs most satisfactorily and who was popular with his several employers. Yet there the family was, on relief. And do you know why, Opal?"

"Nope."

"Opal, because that woman was still essentially a child. Her thriftiness didn't lead her to skimp at the poker table as she did at her dining room table. All for the chips, you might say, and little for the stomachs. Well, the men lost heart when there was no tangible return for their efforts."

"Ah, what a pity."

"Oh, it ended happily," Mrs. Pilger said proudly. "One day I took the woman to the orphanage. She was depressed by the sights she saw, but I pointed out to her quite bluntly that each of those orphans was served three excellent meals a day, that each was receiving a proper education, that each was being given proper training. I then said it might be well to place her boy in such a home, because it was obvious she wasn't doing as much for him as the institution was doing for each orphan. She went ashen. Gambling, if you please, was never again a problem."

"Really?"

Mrs. Pilger looked down at the bowls. All were heaped with salad, the oil gleaming in the sun's afterglow and the light of flickering torches.

"Well," she conceded, "it *was* shock treatment that just happened to be effective. Most gamblers remain gamblers until they drop, of course. Merely illustrating Mrs. Tinston's point. You do have to be a woman, entirely a woman, before you undertake the serious responsibility of marriage."

Now three or four men, led by Mr. Raine, approached the big barbecue pit. Mr. Raine pronounced things "just dandy," and the men picked up long-handled rakes and spread the coals in the pit. About fifteen huge steaks were prepared for the grill and then laid just so over the coals. The sizzling sound and the smells soon brought the party together, and Opal was interested to discover that Mrs. Wentworth was in attendance, a very sassy-looking redhead in cream riding pants and a colorful plaid surcoat. When she could accomplish it without seeming obvious, Opal got to the woman's side in a hurry. "Smell good?" she asked casually. "The Raines are famous for their barbecued beef. Some say it's what they do to the meat before they broil it, and others say it's the type of fuel they use. One of Tincup's more pleasant mysteries."

The famous green eyes took her measure, recognized her. Out came a hand, and Opal pumped it solemnly. "I adore the outdoors," Mrs. Wentworth confided. "I adore the vastness of Texas, the beauty of its evening sky."

"What you ought to do then, Mrs. Wentworth, is ride off some evening and sleep out under the stars. There's an experience you won't ever forget."

"And the beasts?"

Opal had to think a moment before it occurred to her that a city person might actually be afraid of roving coyotes. "Ah," she said, "there's nothing out on the range to harm you. The coyotes may howl rather fiercely, but they're more afraid of you than you of them."

"Would you go with me, do you think?"

"I?"

"Why not? Or hasn't Mr. Lane informed you that we have come to an agreement of a sort? Well, Miss Bondy—no, I shall call you Opal— well, Opal, we have. And isn't it always an excellent idea for a client and a publicist to become well acquainted with one another? Of course!"

"Mike hadn't told me, Mrs. Wentworth."

"Oh, call me Norma. I never could abide formality."

"And has Mike told you, Norma, that the dog-kicking gimmick can't be used now?"

"I was quite furious, of course. It's always clever, I find, to acquire publicity by seeming to espouse some glorious cause such as feeding little children or being kind to dumb animals or battling for cleaner motion pictures or books. The organized groups involved in such activities are always so delighted to have a name in their ranks. So they proceed to use your name in all *their* publicity and give *you* publicity while they're doing so."

Norma Wentworth paused, glanced about.

"Always remember that," she went on. "The difference between small and large publicity firms is that the successful firms know the value of publicity gimmicks that hatch additional publicity indefinitely."

"Mike knows all the tricks," Opal assured her. "Actually, Mike could have an important job in New York or Hollywood. It's just that he prefers Texas life."

"Love him?"

Opal felt her cheeks turn warm, but she stood her ground. "Could be."

"I wouldn't, if I were you. Now don't be angry with me. Aren't we all sisters under the skin? Of course! And I do have a broader experience than you. The Mike Lane type is quite familiar to me. Tall, strong, handsome, made much of, spoiled, corrupted, destroyed. You see many like him in Hollywood."

"But you could be wrong, couldn't you?"

Norma Wentworth laughed that world-famous bubbling chuckle that made you want to laugh along with her. Then three more guests arrived, and two of those guests made just about everyone look at the Raines with increased respect. Sally, the scamp, made much of her social triumph. Off Sally went under the torches, her blonde head gleaming, to say quite warmly and happily:

"About time you folks showed up! Hi, Mr. Prather; hi, Maverick! Welcome to Raine's Jumbled Acres!"

The cattle baron gave her a jovial swat on her britches and yelled for all to hear that there wasn't a tidier ranch in all Texas. His daughter, a veritable blade of intense brunette beauty, gave Sally a kiss on the cheek and gestured for Mike Lane to hand the hostess a big hamper of contributions to the festivities. Maverick fell into step beside Sally, helping her with the big hamper for a time and then picking it up and putting it onto a shoulder and carrying it gracefully the rest of the way to the tables.

Norma gave Opal a sidelong glance. "Lovely child, that. Know her?"

"Nope. Most of us don't know the Prathers. We know of them, naturally, and we gossip more than we should about their affairs. I suppose they're just about the biggest ranch extant, the King Ranch excepted. Have you ever been there?"

"Mr. Prather and my husband are old cronies."

"It must be a fabulous place!"

Norma chuckled. "On the contrary. It's an ordinary adobe ranch house squatting like a pint-size spider in the middle of a web of fences. They have but one servant, an old cowboy who was hurt in some accident years ago. I'm sure the Raines here live much more graciously than the Prathers."

That was difficult for Opal to believe until she saw the easy, convivial, man-to-man way Mr. Bruce Prather was ambling about, shaking hands and chatting with this one and that. His manner certainly wasn't that of a man tremendously impressed or spoiled by his own success. Nor, for that matter, was Maverick's. When Opal went back to the tables in response to Sally's hail, she found Maverick whetting a big butcher's knife with the casual skill of a girl who'd used one all her life. To the introduction, Maverick said: "Howdy." Her handshake was warm, firm. Her smile was genuine. "I've heard of you," Maverick told her. "You're prettier than Mike said. I like that feathery way you do your hair. It doesn't matter a darn how much you wet it, I suppose. Think you'll like ranch life?"

"Ranch life? I hadn't given it much thought."

"Well, you'd better begin. Mike and Dad have cooked up a deal. You're to ride herd on me, or so they think."

"I'm to do *what?*"

Maverick thumbed her finger toward Mike, and Opal, dumbfounded, hustled over to him to repeat her question.

Chapter 4

Mike flatly refused to discuss the matter either that evening at the barbecue or all the following week at the office. He stated it was Opal's job to concern herself solely with assignments and to leave all else related to agency affairs to him. He grew somewhat heated toward the end of the week when she pressed him once more for an answer. "Would you like to quit?" he demanded. "I'm sure you can find more satisfactory employers in town. What about Nutting? The way that character ogles you, he'd give you anything you want to bribe you to an altar."

Opal began to hope it was jealousy that was making him so nasty. But then Mike yelled: "I'm sick and tired of people telling me how to run my business," and her hope died. After he strode out to spend a week in distant Dallas, she did give serious thought to quitting. She could, she thought disgustedly, earn about the same wages slinging hash in Cal's down the road. If her romance with Mike were just an on-again, off-again affair, a little entertainment for him when the emotional going was heavy elsewhere, the sooner she quit the better it would be for her both economically and emotionally.

Feeling angry, discouraged, she discussed the matter with Kitty toward the closing hour on Friday afternoon. There was no formality in the office when Mike was absent, so Kitty slipped off her shoes and made herself comfortable on a corner of Opal's elegant desk. Kitty listened to the nonsense without once interrupting. At the end, Kitty's blonde head described a pert arc. "All the way, Opal," Kitty said. "If I had a boy friend like Mr. Lane, I'd either crack the wrip or drop him over some cliff. You know how many women he has on his string?"

"I've often wondered."

"At least five that I know of. Add about four who'd like to be. Then he's got a mystery gal somewhere. I don't know who she is, but every so often she telephones, and he makes me leave the reception room so I can't listen in."

Opal laughed to indicate she was really quite amused. The big gray eyes watched her, however, as if their owner thought she were insane. Opal stopped laughing.

"Anyway," Kitty said, "I don't get the feeling Mr. Lane has marriage on his mind. A girl gets around and she learns about fellows. Pretty soon she can spot those who are serious and those who are just playing. I never see any seriousness in Mr. Lane."

"And you?" Opal asked.

The girl shrugged. "Fellows like Mr. Lane, Miss Bondy, clown around if you've got a passable face and figure. But he doesn't pay much attention to me. That's something else. It shows that he's got business on his mind first and that everything else comes second. That's what I mean when I say I never see any seriousness in Mr. Lane."

"Well, earning security for your girl and your family is rather serious, you know."

"Nope. First things first, as they say. Until you've got the girl and the family, the security doesn't have to be earned."

A few minutes later, Kitty's boy friend dropped in to say he could get some mounts to ride if Kitty could get out before quitting time. Opal couldn't resist the appealing gray eyes, so girl and boy drove off a few minutes later with happy chatter and laughter that left her feeling much too old and depressed and lonely.

The thing to do, she decided, waiting for five o'clock to arrive, was to drop Mike off that cliff Kitty had mentioned and begin again. Not with Bert, of course, but with someone very handsome and gallant and rich and intellectual and interesting and generous and kind. Surely there were fellows like that still around! With such a fellow, she'd not repeat the major error she'd made early in her relationship with Mike. Veddy, veddy cool she'd play it, the barely approachable iceberg. Did he want to dine her here? Then they'd dine somewhere else! Did he wish a kiss now? But kisses were such a bore!

Ha!

She dropped it there, hearing the door open into the reception room. She went out quickly, smilingly, and found a boy about twelve or thirteen poking his head timidly inside. Her smile apparently reassured him, for all of him came inside, dusty levis, worn boots, dangling-tailed shirt, greasy-looking Stetson being tortured by his hands. Opal said "Hi" as pleasantly as she could, but he wasn't one to be impulsively friendly. He subjected her roundish, lightly tanned face to searching scrutiny. He examined her from head to toe, surely not missing the run in the left stocking or the little smudge of ink on her skirt. Then and only then did he say: "Howdy." As if the word had exhausted his vocabulary, he clasped his hands and the Stetson before him and stood looking at her unwinkingly.

The traffic thickened outside as many of the

workers left for the weekend and the ranchers and their hands came to town for a pleasant respite from the range. The noise of the traffic rose and fell almost rhythmically, reminding Opal for some reason of the surf she'd often heard rising and falling along the shore of distant Long Island in New York State. She supposed that if one were to stand outside an hour or so one would see fully half the registered vehicles of the county either rolling into or out of town. Fine growing town, she thought complacently, and then she looked at the unwinking boy and ventured her second comment.

"Fine day," she said, "isn't it?"

He looked around as if in pain. Understanding, Opal went around Kitty's desk and gave the brass spittoon a little nudge forward with her toe. The tobacco juice hit it nicely. "Thanks," the boy said.

Now, of course, the tempo could be quickened, because she had demonstrated herself to be a hospitable and understanding female critter. Opal sat down and asked: "Anything I can do for you? We close around five."

"Agnew."

"Agnew? Jeb Agnew?"

"Yup."

"What about him?"

"Reckon you know where he's holed."

It was a statement, not a question, Opal noticed.

"Well," she countered, "perhaps I do and perhaps I don't. Do you have business with him?"

"Yup."

"Care to state it?"

"Nope."

The tawny eyes reminded her of wild eyes she'd once seen at just about the same distance from her. There was nothing soft in them. They were terrible in their implacable savagery. Such eyes wouldn't change expression if you bled to death before them, screaming all the way in agony.

A frightening suspicion came into Opal's mind. She asked huskily: "Did you own that dog he kicked?"

"Yup."

"I'm sorry, very sorry."

"Reckon you'll tell me where he's holed."

And again it was a statement, not a question.

"Suppose I did," Opal asked, "what then?"

"Shoot him."

"Really, now!"

"Cain't kick m' hound dog. Ain't fittin'."

"The dog bit him, you know. I'm not taking that up. It's on file at police headquarters."

"Not Daisy."

"Come back Monday," she told him, "and I'll show you the report at the police station."

"Polecat, he'll run."

"Still," she said, "you'd not want to kill an innocent man. That would be unfair."

That hit him. For the first time, the terrible savagery left his eyes. Now the eyes showed bewilderment, concern. "Cain't kill no innocent man," he said. "Ain't fittin'. How come the paper story, though?"

"A big mistake, I'm afraid." Opal went back to her office and got the copy of the *Informer* in which Bert Nutting himself had printed a retraction under his byline. She handed the boy the newspaper and went about the business of closing up while he read. At some time during the procedure, the boy left. The paper, she discovered, had left with him. Automatically she went to the telephone.

The Chief of Police, Mr. Burtis, was just as inclined as she to take the matter quite seriously. "I guess we'll look into it," he said. "You get a lot of these kids running wild on the range who've never heard about law and order. We get shooting out there every so often. Real television Western stuff, Miss Bondy. Those fellows head for the Badlands and hole up until the hunt is called off."

"I told him to come back on Monday."

"You get his name?"

"I'm afraid not."

"Well, we'll investigate, all right. If I was you, I'd tell Agnew to watch out."

Opal thought that a good idea and attended to the chore before she drove home. Jeb Agnew lis-

tened in his chair before the fish pond. He snort-
ed a couple of times, then dismissed the whole
thing as nonsense. "I can take care of myself,"
he snapped. "Any kid takes a pot shot at me, it'll
be his last. I've lived and worked with some
rough characters in my time. Look around this
area some day. When I came here with my first
exploration rig, this was unsettled land. When I
hit the big field, just about every bum and sharp-
shooter in Texas came here hoping to grab it
from me. But you notice Jeb Agnew still owns
what he found, huh?"

"Just following the Chief's orders, sir."

He startled her. "Naturally," he snapped, "I
feel sorry for the kid. If you've got a dog you love,
losin' it is serious. You see him again, you buy
him any dog he wants and bill me."

There was, she discovered, some quality in him
that brought out all the latent tartness in her.
"My," she had to josh him, "can you be develop-
ing a conscience at this late stage in your life?"

The hard blue eyes raked her face. "You got
a sharp tongue, all right. Too bad you ain't got

brains. Let me tell you something. You've got to have everything before you can come to grips with Jeb Agnew. Tongue ain't enough. Brains alone ain't enough. If I tell Lane to fire you, you're fired. If I tell nobody in town to hire you, you ain't hired."

"Oh, I like to think there are many in town who'd tell you to mind your own business, sir."

"But that's what I'd be doing, you see, and that's what they'd be doing by following my orders. You know how much a month I spend in Tincup? Maybe four hundred thousand."

Opal swallowed, rose.

"Sit down," he ordered.

Opal sat down.

He smiled quite pleasantly. "Prather's been asking me about you," he told her. "Got the impression he was putting you on his personal payroll. How come Lane is letting you go?"

"I didn't know he was."

"Would have to be. Prather's like me. We don't lease help; we buy it outright. I told Prather you don't have much brains but that you get things done."

Opal resented the insult but enjoyed the compliment.

"Told him to outline in detail just what he wants done. Told him if he did that, you'd get the thing done the way he wants it."

"And won't upset any applecarts in the process, Mr. Agnew?"

"Paper's been roweling me for years. Sure I wanted them over a barrel. You spoiled that."

"I'm glad I did."

"Why?"

"Because people shouldn't hurt other people."

"What about them hurting me?"

"They shouldn't."

"You tell them that, huh?"

"Gladly."

He wagged his sun-raddled head. "Sunday school stuff, girl. Only one way to go through life: take what you want and stomp them that tries to stop you."

Opal gave up. "Did Mr. Prather say what he expects me to do for him?"

"Nope."

"Well, it doesn't matter, since I won't do it."

"Lane asked me if it was okay to put someone else on my account. I asked why. He said you was leaving to take more profitable work. In that case, I said, all right. So I guess you're leaving Lane, huh?"

At that moment, Opal didn't know why, a shiver ran up the nape of her neck to tingle along her scalp.

Chapter 5

In distant San Antonio, in mid-afternoon of April twentieth, Mike Lane pinned his conscience to the mat by means of some tricky, rather illogical rationalization. The victory inspirited him. He rose from the bed on which he'd lain thinking and smoking for several hours. He showered under cold water, put on fresh slacks and a lightweight jacket, and went down to the lobby of the Blue Bonnet Hotel. Several young ladies, each sitting alone, fortified his belief that Opal Bondy was indeed expendable. One particularly interested him, a striking titian-haired creature, quite tall, exquisitely dressed, possessed of a coolly charming dignity that evoked a memory of a narcissus he'd once seen growing under the tangled confusion of a venerable apple tree. Mike went over to her and asked without preamble or banalities: "Care for lunch, miss? The food here is excellent."

"Like a narcissus before a wind, she moved somewhat but she didn't unbend.

Titillated, Mike reached into his well-stocked bag of tricks. Reasoning that her dignity and her clothes were the products of good breeding, money, and culture, he loosed his conception of an urbane chuckle. "Surely," he said, "a simple offer of lunch is no affront to a civilized lady."

"Thank you, but no."

At that point an ordinary fellow would have bowed politely and left. However, there was a cross-grain in Mike's nature that prevented ready or good-humored acceptance or refusal. He calmly pulled a chair over and sat down and asked quite calmly: "Well, then, would you mind telling me if you bought that bracelet in India? It's quite an unusual bracelet, isn't it? The delicate scrollwork, if that's what you call it, is quite Oriental."

She looked down at her arm in surprise. "Why, I've never asked," she said. "I saw it in Neiman-Marcus one day in Dallas and just bought it."

"There's the place to purchase quality merchandise. I've traveled extensively in Texas recently, and I've been struck by the paucity of quality stores in what you might term the hinterland."

"I would guess it was manufactured somewhere in the Orient," she said. "There's a good luck message engraved in some odd language on the inside. Care to look?"

"Well, if it isn't too much trouble. Frankly, I'm looking for something different to give my fiancé. She has a passion for Oriental jewelry, and when I noticed your bracelet, I—"

"No trouble at all," she assured him. "I think it's the duty of all women to encourage men to buy nice jewelry for their fiancées."

Mike examined the engraving inside the bracelet. He shrugged, laughed. "It could be Hindustani or Shan or Hottentot or even pig Latin," he confessed, "and I'd not know the difference. It's odd, but I have absolutely no talent for languages."

Her eyes twinkled. 'I thought," she said gravely, "that you would translate it into something like *Pishtush loves Mishmush*. Then I would have told you the language is Sanskrit and the message is a warning to beware of strange men possessed of appetite but no luncheon companion."

Oh, that was good! Mike threw his head back and laughed most heartily to show her how terribly good he thought it. He then flung up his hands and rose. "Far be it from me," he told her, "to argue with such a sage. Thank you so much, though, for having allowed me to trouble you."

Came a bow, gracefully executed, then the easy about-face of a well-behaved man about to effect a civilized departure.

But even a narcissus, it developed, could hanker for nourishment and companionship. "I've changed my mind," she informed him. "Lobby sitting or solitary dining can be dreadfully dull."

The simple act of escorting her into the lobby restaurant afforded Mike considerable satisfaction. He told her so with unconscious boyish charm. "It's the honor," he elaborated. "It's a sublime honor for any man to walk with any lady, to have her company even briefly. Two souls in a sea of souls, or two molecules in an infinity of gas. They meet, they share experience. Wonderful! I consider it an honor to share an experience of existence with another."

"What a friendly philosophy!"

"Thanatopsis in reverse, really. Bryant would console you on your deathbed by reminding you that everyone goes and that when you reach your last resting place you'll lie down in good company, with all who have gone before you, the patriarchs, the kings, the powerful, the wise, the good, the fair, and so on. Well, sure, that's an experience shared, but I think I prefer to be at one with mankind while I'm this side of the old crust."

They were taken to a table and were served delicately flavored filet of sole. While they ate,

Mike learned her name was Linda Ann Carter, that her home was in that same Uvalde, Texas, that had given John Nancy Garner to the Vice Presidency of the United States, that her folks grew pecans, that she had just returned from one of those enormously expensive grand tours of the world.

"Have you been abroad?" she asked. "Quite an interesting adventure. I liked England best, particularly the Wordsworth country."

"Fine world," Mike said, neatly evading an answer. "But now what, Miss Carter? Marriage? A career?"

"Marriage, I should imagine."

Yes, he thought dourly, that was the thing they all had in mind. They called it love, they called it natural, they called it completion of oneself, they called it perpetuating the specie, but what it all came down to was self-gratification acquired at the expense of the poor devil who'd be tricked by glowing eyes into believing he was getting the better of the exchange.

Her eyes, startlingly blue, recalled his wandering mind. "I say good luck to you," he told her enthusiastically. "It's the only way of life."

"Your fiancée must be a very nice person."

"The best there is."

"How did you meet her? I'm always curious about the how and why of things."

He laughed and told her, but what began as a simple report on the event was expanded into quite a longish tale, because the words jogged his memory and it was as if the meeting had occurred yesterday, every detail of it so sharp it was queerly like living through it again.

The street at high noon, the air acrid with dust, the sun relentless, the groggy thought Texas was fit for neither man nor beast. The tavern on the corner with the blue sign ornamented by beguiling icicles; the words *Air Conditioned* drawing him inexorably to a round marble-topped table and the solace of cold beer. Nutting, the big fellow, was eating a sandwich and chatting with a slender beauty of such wholesome charm he had to walk over and force an introduction. "Speak of the fellow and here he is," Nutting had said.

"Mike, old man, glad to see you. Miss Opal Bondy, may I present Tincup's outstanding publicist, Michael Lane? Mike, Miss Bondy is a home town girl possessed of a college education and New York training who wants to work in public relations."

Mike grinned at the different beauty at this different table in San Antonio. "So it happened," he said. "I needed a girl possessed of a college education and New York training."

"How odd to think that if the day had been cool you might never have met her!"

"Kismet!"

"That must be so. How else explain the inevitable meeting with the person with whom you'll share most of your life?"

"So it worked out," Mike went on. "She's quite good in her field, incidentally. Opal likes people; there's the secret of her success. About once a day she reminds me that you must like people if you're to be of any use to those who need you."

"Will she work after your marriage, or what?"

It occured to Mike in that moment that he was being hemmed in a bit by that lie he'd told about his fiancée.

"Haven't given it any thought," he said, resorting to the truth. "Well, enough about me. Doing anything this afternoon? I like old San Antone. I liked it the first day I saw it. I like the river meandering through town, I like the park, I like the Spanish influence. Care to stroll about?"

"I think I'd enjoy it."

So, to his pleasure, it was a new beginning in a fine old town on a delightfull balmy day. They walked to the Alamo, and she said how tiny it was and how insignificant it looked dwarfed by all those great stores and buildings. He told her she was measuring bigness with unsuitable calipers. Bigness, he explained, had nothing to do with the physical. Bigness was spiritual. "And consider this," he concluded. "Here we stand where many millions have stood, honoring Bowie and Crockett and all the others who fought here for the ideal of freedom. But have other millions come to this Plaza to honor those who built those stores that appear to reduce this fort to insignificance?"

They walked on and found the river flowing like molten copper through the business district. A few steps down to the walkway, to the fresh green plantings, to the gurgling of the water, and it was as if they'd stepped into an older, more peaceful, more charming world. Mike took her hand. He took it without nonsense and gave it a squeeze and said: "This is more like it. Care to sit?"

She said that would be nice, it was so very lovely there. But of course a couple of boys came along, and one happened to find a rather sizable twig that could be utilized as a toy boat. The boat was launched. The boat came a cropper. One of the boys came running to Mike. "*Señor*," he said, "*por favor*, you unsink the boat?"

"Scoot," Mike ordered. "Go over to the park if you want to play."

"But *señor!*"

Mike rose half threateningly, and the boys ran off.

"Never could stand Mexicans," Mike said. "I squirm every time I meet them."

"Really? I have many dear Mexican friends. May I ask a question, Mike?"

"Sure."

"Well, why this? What's the reason for it or, better still, what's the necessity behind it? I've been asking myself that question for several hours. You're engaged. And yet . . . ?"

"Life," he said, feeling quite confident now. "Anyway, a fellow does get lonely."

"When did you decide not to marry her, Mike?"

He started. He stared.

She smiled ever so faintly, and so beautifully he was touched. "It was too illogical to be convincing," she explained. "I mean, your tongue was saying one thing, but those savage black eyes were saying other things. You know what I think?"

"What."

"You want things as you want them. You wanted solitude here, so you weren't reluctant to threaten those children into flight. And you effect your pickups so very skillfuly one must logically think you've had much practice. All of which means what? Well, you quite obviously like to play, so I think you decided not to marry her because marriage would be inconvenient. Right?"

"You do considerable thinking up there, don't you?"

"Naturally. One must. And in this case it is probably just as well. Spares you time and money, and spares me considerable effort and boredom."

"Boredom?"

She laughed harshly and snapped her fingers in his face. "You conceited popinjay, you. Did you honestly think your approach was so different and so convincing? My dear fellow, there's not a woman on earth who can't give you better lines without trying. Of course I was bored. But work is work, and I did have to listen and endure it until I was sure it was merely the old chase after conquest needed by an obviously wobbly conceit.

All right. The name is my correct name, but I'm a police detective, Mike. There've been some pickups in this section of town lately, with theft at the end of the ball. You may leave."

"Show me your badge," he challenged. "Go ahead."

She showed him her badge.

Jolted, Mike returned alone to the hotel and went up to his room to pack. Women, he thought sourly, couldn't be trusted.

Chapter 6

Opal smiled pleasantly enough Sunday afternoon when Mike Lane opeend the gate of the split-rail fence before her home. "Ma," she called, "ice up a coke-punch special."

Her mother called back testily that there couldn't be visitors inasmuch as her daughter wasn't dressed to receive visitors. Her mother enlarged on this theme just inside the front screen door. "Of course if you're just trying to sell your legs, Opal, I suppose those shorts are appropriate. But when *I* was a girl and had a Sunday afternoon visitor, I received that visitor dressed as a lady ought to dress."

Opal swatted at her knee. The fly went away

but returned, obviously attracted by the purple-red abrasion on her kneecap. "You have any bear grease?" she asked. "I make no complaint. Pain comes, pain goes; but I would like to frustrate this fly."

Mike completed the long walk from the gate to the deep front porch. He smiled at Opal's mother and sat down beside Opal and told her he'd missed her and was delighted to be home once more. "We have a fine town here," he said soberly. "The name isn't much and our early history is nothing to brag about, but we have a fine and growing town here. I think that every time I return from a trip. Dallas and Houston and San Antonio are too large now. You need space around you, earth, sky, trees, stock, if you want to derive the best from Texas living."

"We got the account to boost Tincup, then?"

He gave her a disapproving glance.

"Sounded like it," she defended herself. "And I knew you were badgering the Chamber of Commerce to let you direct the boost-Tincup campaign."

"Is there anything about my business that you don't know?" he asked sarcastically.

"A few things. For example, I don't know why I'm to be shunted off to ranch life at this season of the year. What have I done to merit this prize assignment? In what way have I unknowingly contrived to measure up to your high standards of efficiency?"

"One more crack," he said, "and I'm walking on."

"To which fair beauty, sir?" Will it be Alice or Betty or Kitty? Now I recommend Kitty. Her eyes are gray. They'll remind you of the eternal sea, the peace of the sea, its kinetic beauty under some beamish moon."

"What's wrong with you?" he demanded. "I come home worn out from a difficult trip and you give me a welcome such as this. What's wrong? What's bothering you?"

"My vanity has been mangled. I thought I did a pretty fair job there at the office. I never expected to be dumped."

"Who said you're dumped?"

"Jeb Agnew. Maverick Prather."

It rocked him. Glaring straight ahead, he yelled: "People should mind their own business. I hate wagging tongues."

Opal took it well. Nothing in her expression or her manner indicated he'd just shattered her last carefully treasured hope. "It's the sociability of country folks," she told him. "Your affairs are important to them because there aren't too many affairs to analyze. The word 'your' is used in a general way, incidentally."

Mrs. Bondy brought a pitcher of coke-punch special out to the porch. On her second trip she brought glasses, cheese and crackers, and a jar of some fragrant salve. She told Mike to help himself. She got down on her knees and opened the scratches with firm movement of her fingers. Her daughter's exaggerated yelps and writhings were ignored. The salve was smeared on and worked down into each scratch. A dressing was produced and taped over the abrasion. "I always knew," Mrs. Bondy bragged, "that my first-aid training would be useful one day. Feels better, eh?"

Mike arched his brows. "Dog bite *you?*"

"Speaking of dogs," Opal told him, "the boy who owned the dog Mr. Agnew kicked came to the office to find out where the polecat is holed up. Objective: gunplay."

"Say, that's serious! Tell the police?"

"Certainly. But the boy didn't come back on Monday, as I expected him to. It was after I'd reported the danger to Mr. Agnew that he told me I was being dumped."

Mike finished his punch and set the glass on the floor. "The fact is you're not being dumped. Oh, sure, you'll work for Prather, take orders from Prather, draw pay from Prather. But your connection with the firm continues in a sort of suspended form. What happened is this. Prather had need of this personal type of service. I could have refused him, sure. After all, we don't run what amounts to a nursing service. But you don't develop into a nationwide organization without clients like the Prathers. You need those fat accounts, business you can depend upon year in and year out. I thought if I humored him in this, he might throw us some of his business problems to handle. Quite reasonable, if you ask me."

"Except for one thing," Opal corrected him mildly. "I'm a publicist, not a nurse."

"Simple assignment, Opal. And perhaps I used the wrong term to describe your function there. The nub of the thing is that Prather approves of Tate Craithorne and wants him for a son-in-law. Craithorne is interested in Maverick Prather, all right, but the traditional proposal is never uttered."

"Perhaps the field is more beguiling than the individual?"

"No sarcasm; this is business!"

"Merely an observation," Opal said dryly.

"Prather had figured out that it's Craithorne's family that prevents the marriage. And he could be right. Pick up almost any issue of the *Informer* and you'll find the Craithorne family on the society page. And Maverick isn't society, to put it mildly."

"That lovely girl? Don't be silly, Mike!"

"That lovely girl, Opal, can ride any bronc

they own, throw any steer she can rope, haze stock from the brush with a helicopter, and shoot out the eye of a gnat at thirty paces. In short, she's not been broken to décolletage, pumps and the ballroom."

"Why should that matter? This isn't Dallas or New Orleans or San Francisco or Philadelphia, you know. This is Tincup—cattle country, oil country, a place to work, not a place to dance."

"It matters enough to Prather so that he'll pay you six hundred a month and found to ride herd on Maverick, teach her the social graces, transform her into a reasonable facsimile of a society lady."

The sum took Opal's breath away. With money such as that to work with, a girl could do many things. She could have the old homestead air-conditioned. She could refurnish the place. She could even treat her folks to a grand tour to see all the sights on the North American continent.

Mike smiled faintly. "Real dirty trick of me to dump you, isn't it?"

Yet despite the raillery there was something

in his manner that troubled her. She couldn't pinpoint it, couldn't define it; yet it was real enough to fill her with odd disquietude. "I'll think about it," she said politely. "How long do I have?"

"You have no job at the office now, so it would cost you if you took too long to make up your mind."

"Who handles my work?"

"Oh, I found someone in Houston who seemed possible."

"That explains the trip, I dare say?"

"Houston, Dallas, San Antonio," he said with a shrug. "A lot of real estate to cover just to find the right type of assistant. You'll like Ann Addie. You're about the same age, but she's about two years behind you, professionally speaking."

"Lovely?"

Mike Lane laughed unabashedly. "You always ask that sarcastically. I wonder why? Listen, Opal. It's quite normal for a fellow to see beauty and to be drawn toward it. Of course she's lovely! I'd not have less in the office if I had any choice in the matter. But I haven't dated her, I'm not in love with her, and I'm not intending to add her to my long list of great conquests."

"Fine. In that event, send her to the ranch. Excellent idea. Mr. Agnew's work requires know-how, and—"

"That's the deal," Mike interrupted. "Now if you don't mind, I think I'll go home and sleep a week. Don't bother to come in to clear out your desk. We'll send your personal things to you and turn the business things over to Ann."

Opal waited until he'd walked halfway down the steps. She then said crisply and clearly: "Nope."

Mike halted and swung around.

"You can fire me, of course," Opal conceded. "But you can't force me to accept a job I don't want. I'll call Bert in the morning. He's been badgering me for some time to let him find me a real job. I suspect I now toil for Tincup's sole department store. Ah, well, it'll be an experience."

He stood there a long time, still as death, his gaze unwinking, his cleft chin thrust forward grimly. But there was no tantrum, no resort to savagery of any kind. "As you wish," he muttered. "I thought the firm's success meant something to you, but if it doesn't, that's that."

And in the heat of Sunday afternoon, with insects whirring and not a tree stirring, he walked away.

She got the door open and went inside. Her father came out of the living room and gave her a little wink and then went outdoors. Her mother also came out of the living room to ask with a grin: "Want a shoulder to sob on, dearest?" But it was all right. It took a moment to establish control over her nerves, and then the situation could be carried off with a reasonable show of aplomb.

"Actually," Opal said, "it's been obvious a long time, Ma. You kid yourself, yet you don't. You say he's just having some fun, yet deep down you know a guy really in love will seek that fun with his darling. So bit by bit you prepare yourself for the inevitable moment of truth, and it really doesn't hurt as much as most think."

"Fine. You ought to have a nap and rest that knee, I think. Did I remember to tell you the

Chapter 7

Opal remained home a week; then the house and inactivity became boring. She looked around her bedroom one morning and decided that if she spent another minute inside it that day she'd scream. She changed into a linen ensemble, got her car from the garage, and drove to Independence Avenue to find a job. It seemed to her that an oil company would be a good bet. People were always criticizing oil companies for making too much money, demanding too many special tax concessions from the government, making too many sub rosa deals with undesirable big shots in Africa, Asia, and everywhere else. If an oil company didn't need a publicist, she reasoned,

who did?

The personnel manager of the first oil company she tried was interested in her point of view. He said rather amusedly: "You sound like a district attorney making out a case against a scoundrel, Miss Bondy. Oh, I suppose there are people who deplore our existence, our operations, our profits, or even all three. But there have always been malcontents, and not even you will change that."

"But a good publicist can change the opinions of many, sir."

"Conceded. But what we're not agreed upon, Miss Bondy, is the quality of your work and training. Now as I see your application, you're a relative beginner. You went to college and were an A student. Excellent. You went to New York and worked for a time for an insurance company. Excellent. You returned to Tincup to work for Mr. Lane. Not so excellent. The fact is, Miss Bondy, that a publicist can acquire little valuable experience in a small firm such as Lane's; experience useful to an organization such as ours, I mean. Most of Lane's accounts are short-term accounts, ad hoc accounts, you might say. But we have programs, Miss Bondy, long-range programs designed for the purpose of acquiring long-range benefits. And it's in this specific area, the area of sustained effort over a period of years, that you are weak. You see?"

"Mr. Agnew isn't small, sir, and the firm does have his account."

"Ah, yes. But what do people of Tincup think of Jeb Agnew? What do outsiders think of him? I think his public image, Miss Bondy, reflects no credit on Lane. Do you know our Mr. Cavanaugh?"

Opal ransacked her memory but couldn't place the name. Her "I'm afraid not, sir," brought a glint of triumph to the man's eyes. "There's my point," he said. "Mr. Cavanaugh is our majority stockholder, a man easily worth a hundred million. A thoroughly dissolute, despicable man, Miss Bondy. He has an island off Mexico on which he lives in great opulence. One day a reporter thought Mr. Cavanaugh would make an excellent subject for a magazine article. The reporter went to the island, with a camera, without permission. The camera was smashed and tossed into the ocean. The reporter was severely beaten by several of Mr. Cavanaugh's guards. Indeed, he was almost killed. And yet, Miss Bondy, you have never heard of our Mr. Cavanaugh, and I doubt there are a hundred persons in the United States who know of his wealth, his power, his delusions of grandeur."

Opal got the point. "I understand, sir. At any rate, thanks for the interview."

Her next stop brought her face to face with a short, chunky, sharp-eyed woman with a mane of gray hair wore in mannish style. "Ah, yes," the woman said. "I know of you, Miss Bondy. You planned and coordinated a fashion show I once attended. Do sit down. What sort of job did you expect; what sort of salary do you want; what sort of assignments are you after?"

Opal grew a bit hopeful at this point. To tip the scales still further in her favor, she said quickly and succinctly: "Any publicity work; you name the salary; you choose the assignments."

Blunder!

"I hate people," the woman said, "who come looking for work but leave it up to me to determine what their specialties are and what their financial needs may be."

"Sorry," Opal said. "For a hundred a week I'll undertake to do whatever needs to be done."

"Satisfaction guaranteed?"

"Yes."

"Silly statement, Miss Bondy. One of our vice presidents must deliver an address to a geological society tomorrow afternoon. Quite technical. What do you know of geology?"

"Nothing, I'm afraid."

"Then you mustn't guarantee that whatever you undertake to do for a hundred a week will be satisfactory. We like careful thinking in this firm, Miss Bondy. But no matter. Even if your answers had been satisfactory, we'd not have offered you a post. Insufficient experience. My dear young lady, this is the big time. We can and do employ top publicists, each of them a specialist in some area of the publicist's profession. You offer nothing but a severely limited general experience."

"But—"

"Oh, no. No argument, please. There the facts are in your application, and facts must be the basis for our decision."

Opal went on to the next stop. Here she was given the "Well, well, dear, and how are you?" treatment, so she went on to stop number four. Her interviewer this time was a tall, spare man with a deeply tanned face and an outdoors look to his gray eyes. "Any luck elsewhere?" he asked. "You have that tired-applicant look."

"None, sir."

"Inexperience, eh?"

"Inexperience. And that's odd, if I may say so, because a publicity problem is a publicity problem whether it's generated in a big oil corporation or in a corner grocery store. And it seems to me that a person who has acquired broad general experience ought to be given credit for resourcefulness, adaptability, and a high level of professional competence. Also, I think the fact that most of the accounts I've served were small accounts ought to be given weight. If you have a big publicity budget and the prestige of a big corporation going for you, it's quite simple to get whatever form of publicity you wish. But if you have no budget to speak of, no prestige going for you . . ."

"Agnew said no, you see."

It took half a minute for Opal to understand. When the inevitable flush hit her cheeks, he shrugged. "We'll go along with Agnew, too, I'm sorry to say. Agnew's a clever cuss. Somewhere along the line he found out he could make big money with less bother if he just peddled his oil to the industry instead of going into the manufacture and retail sale of oil products. We buy a lot of stuff from him in crude form every month. Can't afford to displease a supplier."

"Did he say why, sir?"

"Nope."

"Would it be the same, do you suppose, if I tried at other than oil firms?"

"Yup, if the outfit's big enough to need a publicist. Sorry, Miss Bondy. I suppose I should have kept quiet, but I can't stand seeing a critter wearing itself out trying to do something hopeless."

"You're very kind, sir."

He shrugged again and stood up as she left.

Down on the street, Opal's first inclination was to have at Mr. Jeb Agnew forthwith. But before she could even go back to her car, it occurred to her the battle would be a waste of energy and time. She tried out a few business firms, got nowhere, and then drove back to her home on Hackberry Street. She shook her head in reply to her mother's questioning look and went straight upstairs to her typewriter. She banged out a four-page account of her job-hunting experiences that day, knocked off to shower and eat, then returned to her bedroom desk to edit and rewrite extensively. When she thought she had what she wanted, an objective and factual story calculated to lift a few eyebrows, she telephoned Bert at his home and asked if he could use a controversial little feature. Bert grandly announced he could always use a feature, controversial or not, and told her to show him the piece in the morning.

He reached for it avidly when she laid the manuscript envelope on his desk promptly at nine o'clock. "Sit down," he invited, "or are you one of those sensitive souls who can't stand the pain of an editorial reading?"

Opal sat down and aimed her gaze at the gray sky visible through the window. Despite his little grunts and sighs, she kept her gaze aimed at the sky until he said: "Nope, couldn't use it if you paid me to print it."

"Why not?" she asked, meeting the big brown eyes. "All of it is true."

"But you couldn't prove it without costing some fellow his job. You wouldn't want to do that, would you?"

"Of course not, but—"

"Want a job here?"

"Doing what?"

"I'll think of something. You have to learn about writing, that's obvious, so you'd definitely not be a reporter. But your experience in public relations ought to be useful. We might work out something for you in the advertising department.

We don't get the ads we should, probably because most of the businesses in town are field offices of national concerns who think of us as suppliers rather than consumers. I think that if we conducted a campaign to make the local firms more ad conscious, we could improve our business ten or twenty percent."

"What would be the use?" she asked unhappily. "If Mr. Agnew can prevent me from getting a job in my field, he can certainly prevent local firms from giving me enough business to justify my salary."

"But he'd be bucking the *Informer* then, you see. That makes it a different kind of battle. Look, I don't discuss my war experiences as a rule, but I have a point to make, so I'll break my rule this once. In the early days of the war, the North Koreans had little difficulty pushing our tiny and unprepared forces right down to the sea. They were stronger, they had the advantage of initiative and preparation. But when we evened things up somewhat, we had no difficulty pushing them back, and we had defeated them by the time the

Chinese sent their so-called volunteers in to help them. Okay. You're in the position our tiny and unprepared forces were in. You can't push a tank back with your bare hands, and you can't lick Agnew without money or conections. Because Agnew knows that, he isn't averse to battling you. But would the North Koreans have started the scrap if they'd known we'd come back with bigger and better tanks? Nope. And Agnew might very well change his mind about battling you if he had to battle us, too."

"But if I were a Sarah Jones, just another name to you, would you still hire me, Bert?"

"Yup."

"Well, how come that vacancy exists; why hasn't it been filled long before this?"

He scowled. Finally he said: "All right, I happen to like you, even love you, and that's a part of this. Just the same, I'd help anyone who was getting a raw deal. I don't happen to think that anyone has the right to push someone else around."

She had to feel impressed. Looking at him, she

had to wonder why in the world she'd not been able to find the eternal magic in him. A big, healthy, good-looking, right-thinking fellow; a man who'd be a darned fine husband to the woman who married him. Compare Mike to him, and—

Sally, entering, broke the thought, the delicate moment. "Your Ma called," she told Opal, "very excited. You know who dropped by to pay you a visit? Rancher named Prather, that's all."

"It almost lifted Opal from the chair.

"More," Sally said, holding up a hand. "Very mysterious message, but your Ma said it'd make sense to you. She says that Mr. Prather said you should try on Independence Avenue again. Did your Ma guess right? Does that make sense to you?"

Opal looked at Bert. Bert looked down at her little feature and proceeded to tear it to bits. "I'd guess," he said thoughtfully, "that a chat with Prather is in order. It'll make him happy, Agnew happy, Lane happy, and what do you have to lose?"

"I just don't like to be forced to do something I don't want to do, Bert. And I don't think I owe Mike that much consideration."

Bert obviously liked that, but he was a man who could concentrate upon the big thing when he thought he should. "If a person helped Prather in a time of need, Opal, that person would have all the tanks and guns she needed from that moment on. Does that make sense to you, too?"

It made sense to her. She didn't know how she was going to accomplish it, but she did know that one fine day both Mr. Jeb and Mr. Mike Lane would be made to wish they'd not tried to push her around.

She nodded at Bert and Sally. Her blue eyes twinkling, she headed downstairs to the street.

Chapter 8

Mr. Bruce Prather said: "Glad to see you, Miss Bondy," and casually waved her to a chair. He sat down himself with the easy manner of a man who had the world by the tail on a downhill pull. "Enjoy the trip out?" he asked. "I never tire of the range. I know every inch of this range, including that part of it over in the Badlands. Acre for acre, I'll match my place with any place in Texas."

"It swallows you," Opal said quite seriously. "After a while I began to feel very small and helpless."

"And you are. We all are. You forget that in your cities, because you don't see the bigness of the world there. Every time I get to feeling mighty important, I saddle up and ride out there and look at the big sky and the big land, and pretty soon I stop feeling too big for my britches. But don't ever let the land frighten you, Miss Bondy. If you have savvy, you can find all you need on the land to sustain life."

"But if you lack savvy, Mr. Prather, the land almost breaks you and you end up teaching your daughter to avoid the land as she would a tiger."

He smiled faintly. "And that's why you told Lane no, I take it? Good enough for me, Miss Bondy. I'm not Agnew. I don't take it as a personal insult if someone I want to hire doesn't want to hire out to me. When Agnew bragged he was driving you to my corral, I worked the telephone. You can return to Lane or you can work in two different oil outfits."

"That was kind of you, sir."

He shrugged. "Fair's fair, it seems to me. But to go on being fair, Miss Bondy, I don't think you can do as much good for yourself in town as you can here. You know my proposition; Lane tells me he outlined it to you. But ride on beyond that. An outfit like mine always has a good responsible job for someone who's proved she's worth her beans. Which would you rather be: just another hand in a big business outfit or ramrod of your own operation here?"

"Ramrod, of course."

He nodded. Now he settled back in his chair, not a big man but a man with a big, forceful personality. Like his daughter, he had brown hair and eyes. Unlike his daughter, however, he was quite homely with his big, slightly askew nose and a scar running from left temple to chin. He said after a moment: "Then we can do business, I think. You want something, I want something, and such folks can always do business. I'll put another blue chip in the pot, making it seven hundred and found. If you can't rope the critter, no complaint, as long as you honestly try."

"But didn't it ever occur to you, sir," Opal had to say, "that a young fellow in this day and age would marry if he wished to regardless of what his folks said?"

"You know what Tate Craithorne has in his pocket, Miss Bondy? Nothing his folks don't put there."

"Still . . ."

"Speaking confidentially," he went on, "that doesn't matter to me. A fellow like me works for two things, his daughter and his pride. Wouldn't matter a hoot to me if I had to pay their expenses or invent a big job for him to handle. But Maverick, she sees it different. She asks how come I think I have to buy her a husband? She says how come I think she'd marry a fellow who couldn't stand on his own two feet?"

"Good for her."

"Sure. But that don't get Maverick a Mrs. in front of her name, and that don't get Craithorne after the Mrs."

"And it must be Tate Craithorne?"

Drumming hoofs sounded outside. Opal looked out the window, and her heart all but leapt up her throat. Coming in flat and hard from the range was the biggest and blackest mount she'd seen in her life, a giant of a horse that cleared a four-foot fence as if it were an insignificant pebble. Crouched on his back sat Maverick Prather herself, dusty, her hair wind-blown, screeching every inch of the way.

"Crazy critter," her father growled. "She rides like that once too often, she'll get her neck broken, and then what? But you can't talk to that girl. Just like her mother. Crazy for the outdoors, for hard riding. Time she was married and settled down."

Maverick hopped down from the mount. She studied Opal's car, then clapped the black on the rump and came striding into the office building with a pleasant jingling of spurs. Her brown eyes danced when she saw Opal sitting there in a neat, immaculate cotton dress. "Hi," she said easily. "Wondered if you'd ever get out here, Opal. Bet Pop a buck you wouldn't."

"Pay me," he ordered.

"Rack it up," she flashed back. "So this is the dude lady who's to rope me, eh? Pop, you ought to be ashamed. In town, folks say she's a nice girl for a city girl."

Their eyes locked. It seemed to Opal that a warning was being given and rejected, and for some reason the whole thing made her uneasy. Deliberately, to establish something, she told Maverick in casual tones: "If I wish to rope and tie you, young lady, I will. Now scoot. Your father and I are conducting a business conversation."

It was difficult to tell who had been jolted most. The girl swung around and the father flung his head back. Both stared as at a garter snake that had suddenly become a rattler.

"Whoa," Maverick said. "Big talk from little brave, Miss Bondy, no offense intended."

"For example," Opal told her sweetly, "I would accept the job only if I were given full authority over you. And if I were given that authority, young lady, you would ride only if I said you could. You see?"

"And if I rode anyway?" the girl asked jeeringly.

"Ah," Opal laughed, "you mustn't expect me to divulge all my tricks, Miss Prather. I haven't accepted the post, you see."

But it told. Despite the girl's cocky chuckle, it told. The girl swung back to her father and said: "It won't work, Pop. Here and now I warn you, it won't work. I'm not a baby. I have the right to my own life. You don't cram me into dresses and girdles and stockings against my will, and you don't—"

"Or what?" Opal asked. "Are you threatening to leave, Miss Prather? For what destination, for what kind of life? Can you earn a living as a cowgirl? Can you romp around the world as you do this range? Out in that world can you have everything as you want it because you're the daughter of Bruce Prather?"

"Just the same—"

"Never make threats," Opal advised her, "you can't make good. That's kid stuff. You're not a kid."

The girl blinked. It was quite clear that no one had ever before dismissed her remarks so contemptuously, and it was also quite clear that she was momentarily confused. Her father didn't miss that. He turned to Opal, wagging his head. "Salary, found, authority, future," he said crisply. "But if you say no, tell me what outfit to call and I'll cancel out Agnew's remarks."

Maverick marched out, her face lobster-red. She mounted the huge black and rode off at a headlong gallop, and you could mark her progress across the range by the flying dust the horse kicked up.

"Whether it's Craithorne or nobody," her father said, "she's gotta be broken, sort of. I made a mistake with her, Miss Bondy. A man left alone with a girl to raise and a ranch to run—well, what can he do? He does his best, but he leaves out a lot. And she always got such fun out of cowboy stuff. She'd ask to go out on roundup, and how could I say no? And the hands are like folks the world over—show 'em a lonesome kid and they'll be right nice to it. Only ten isn't nineteen, is it, and when you're nineteen you're too old to play, aren't you? What I mean is this: how can she take over from me, run this place, if she's allowed to be a kid as long as I'm around?"

"Friends? Girl friends, I mean?"

"None. Used to have a few, but she played tricks on them, like giving them ornery mounts to ride. I better warn you here and now about that. Maverick knows all the dirty tricks. She wasn't taught them deliberately, but you know how fellows are, and her eyes never missed nothing."

"Sounds like fun, sir."

Her twinkling eyes interested him. He laughed. "You like a challenge, then?"

"All public relations work is a challenge, Mr. Prather. Can you meet this problem or that? If you can, you get ahead professionally. And it's fun to try to meet them as they come along."

"Take the job, then?"

Opal hesitated, knowing darned well that this was the biggest problem she's ever tackled. But then it occurred to her that if she couldn't handle this problem she couldn't handle any big problem, and she decided the time had come to learn what she could or couldn't do.

"I'm very happy to accept the job," she told him.

He nodded and pumped her hand. He led her

across a fairly large lawn to the ranchhouse, bawled for somebody named Shorty. Presently a runt of an oldster came limping around from the back of the house. The introductions and explanations were dealt with briskly, and Shorty was then ordered to show the new hand her quarters. But at that point, his lips pursed, Bruce Prather paused. "Nope," he said, "that came out wrong, Shorty. What you should have been told is that Miss Bondy runs the house now, you and the house along with Maverick. She gives you an order, it's the same as if I did. If she doesn't like the room I picked out, let her choose one she does like."

Shorty said: "Ain't workin' for no female, Boss."

Mr. Prather grinned. "Old-timer," he said, "don't you give me any trouble. I've had enough to do sticking this down Maverick's craw, and you know it."

Shorty scowled but led Opal into the house. They passed through an enormous living room, and Shorty explained the layout of the place. All the rooms to the right of the living room were bedroms and bathrooms, and all the rooms to the left of the living room amounted to his territory.

"I like it the way it is," Shorty said belligerently, "and I won't stand for havin' nothin' changed. I ain't sayin' you can't come in there an' give me orders, but anybody I work for has t' let me set things up my own way."

"Does everyone here insist upon having things his own way?"

He pondered that all the way to the end of the hall. Finally he said: "Well, I aim t' be reasonable; no harm in that." He then ushered her into a spacious bedroom. "Fancy?" he asked. It was evident that he'd worked for hours to clean everything and arrange the furniture just so, for he looked about the place with a proud air. "Boss thought all them fancy doodads was what a woman wants," he said, "an' I guess they do look durn pretty. But there ain't nothin' like a deep leather chair when it's sittin' easy you want t' do, so I sort of left that there for you."

"Why, it's beautiful, Shorty! Just beautiful."

"Bed an' curtains was my idea, too. Ever notice how all them stores show spreads an' curtains that match? Silly. Gotta have variety, just like in nature, see? Ain't every tree the same green, huh? I kind of thought them two different greens was okay."

It was an effort, but Opal managed to say she thought they were okay, too. At once the air was cleared. Now Shorty couldn't say enough or do enough to prove he was happy to have such a reasonable and intelligent boss. He suggested that she take a snooze while he got her gear from town. Later on, he said, he'd saddle up a nice horse for her and then he'd take her on a tour of inspection. "Girl," he said, becoming more and more excited, "you won't see nothin' on earth t' beat the first sight you'll get of the Prather herd. If they was all t' stampede at the same time, they'd shake the earth. Comin' together now, girl, on account of roundup. You sure got yourself here at the right time."

"Fine. But I'd better telephone my folks, Shorty. Incidentally, you might have a telephone extension installed here."

He led her back to the living room, and she made the call, and a few minutes later he drove off.

Chapter 9

Putting first things first, Opal spent a full week looking over the Diamond B-P spread, getting acquainted with its hands and hierarchy, adjusting herself to the easygoing tempo of ranch life. Her first day she rode south under a hot and brilliant sun to a neatly subdivided area devoted entirely to the raising of prize registered stock. About halfway to the first fence, she overtook a young redheaded fellow mounted on a white mule. The fellow was dozing along but woke with a start as she came alongside him. He grinned and said "Howdy" and thumbed his Stetson in approved television style. "Ted Thompson," he introduced himself. "You that awful female which has t' be shot?"

"Could be," Opal conceded gravely. "I hope, though, that the shooting here is poor. It's quite an experience to be here. I've never seen such a lovely stretch of country. So much of the land around Tincup is arid. How is the grass kept so green?"

"Took doing," he said, making the understatement of the year. "I come here as a tadpole, so I know. Them days, a army of hands was doing nothing but building dams, changing waterways, drilling all the time for more water. Over there near them hills, we got us a regular old lake now, proving what Mr. Prather always says about the land giving you only what you put into it. So we got grass. Lady girl, we got more kinds of grass than most folks ever heard about. We got buffalo grass and we got bluestem grass and we got Indian grass and we got switch—" Her laughter cut him short. "Well," he said, grinning, "we got grass."

Opal didn't contest it. For as far as she could see in any direction, there stretched grass, some pale green, some deep green, some tall and spiky and golden. As a breeze rippled through the grass, she had the illusion of riding along over a great green-gold sea. The sweet grass smells wafted to her nostrils invigorated her deliciously.

Ted Thompson opened the first gate they came to, waved her through, fastened the gate behind them. "This here mule," he said, "is mine. The boys is always saying some day he'll kick me straight to Kingdom Come, and he sure can be ornery when he has a mind to be. But you take a mule and you got a smart mount under you. Don't never have to teach this mule the same thing twice. Like at that gate. First time I tried opening and closing that gate with him doing the backing and pulling, he throwed me 'most as high as yonder cloud. Well, him and me we had it out. 'Mule,' I said to him, 'you see this here rock? Well, this here rock is gonna bounce off your head next time.' Mule, he kinda looks over this here rock, and now a old lady with a headache can sit on this here mule an' open an' close any gate she wants, an' he'll back an' pull so easy her headache won't get no worse."

Ted Thompson gestured toward a long, low, nicely painted barnlike structure in the distance. "Over there," he said, "is the hogs. We raise white Yorkshire hogs here. Can't stand 'em myself, but there is some that say ain't nothing better to raise than hogs."

Opal spent the balance of that day examining hogs and admiring hogs and learning much about hogs from an old Arkansas hand who could and did speak of hogs with downright passion.

Her second day she rode east in the general direction of the Badlands. For perhaps half a mile the ride was easy and agreeable, and then she passed beyond the grass line to a world of brush and rocks and goats, a land deeply fissured with arroyos and studded with vicious-looking cactus. It was while she was heading back to the ranchhouse that she saw Maverick for the first time since the girl had angrily left the office building. Astride her giant black, her Stetson shoved well back on her head, Maverick rode over to meet her as she came down from

father's idea, not yours. You're just another mouth looking for food your brains will have to earn for it. I apologize for that scene the other day."

"I'd already forgotten it, Maverick."

"In anything reasonable," Maverick said, "I'll cooperate. A girl gets tired of just men. It'll be nice to have you around. Only it'll have to be reasonable."

"What do you call reasonable?"

"Well, this kitchen and clothes and dust-the-window-ledge stuff is plumb crazy! Wouldn't it make as much sense if I were to tell you that you have to learn pronto how to throw and brand a wild calf? What I mean is, some learn this and some learn that, and there's a place for each in this world."

"I didn't know I was to teach you such things, Maverick."

"What's your job, then?"

Opal had to laugh and shake her head. "So help me Hannah," she said, "it's all as vague to me as it is to you. What it amounts to, I suppose, is that your father believes you've played cowboy long enough, and that he hopes my sweet influence, the example I set, will incline you to want to be a woman in fact as well as in name."

"Then Mr. and Mrs. Craithorne will decide I'm good enough for Tate?"

"Aren't you good enough for Tate?"

A queer thing happened. Maverick flushed and spun her horse around as if to gallop off. Then the girl slid lithely to the ground and headed for a pool of shade in the lee side of a great butte. After Opal had joined her there, Maverick shrugged. "Guess not," she said laconically. "You ever see the Craithorne place?"

"No."

"Big house, three stories, with columns and fancy work and porches and what not. Tate says you see many such houses on old Southern plantations. Inside, all the furniture is old and very valuable and elegant. Tate has a library bigger than the public library in Tincup, or almost. Music room. One room is an art gallery. And

Tate's at home there. I mean, all that furniture means something to him and is part of him. The same with the books, the piano, the paintings. He can talk about all of them the way I talk about stock. Well, I can't talk about any of them and don't care to."

"And you think for that reason you're not good enough?"

Maverick shrugged.

Opal waited a few minutes, thinking it over, swabbing her damp face once more. Finally her mind caught up with her instincts and she asked the question her instincts had asked almost from the beginning. "Who's the real love?" she asked. "I mean, the fellow your father doesn't know about?"

Maverick never quivered. "Funny sort of question."

"I have the edge here," Opal fenced back. "I've grown up with hundreds of girls, Maverick, and I think I know girls better than you. You were quick and you were glib, and I'm sure none of the fellows on this ranch would ever doubt you're grieving inwardly because of unrequited love. But girls, you see, listen to *all* the words, and they observe the face of the speaker while the words are pouring forth. You said, for instance, that you don't care to talk of books or music or paintings. Yet a girl in love, eager to marry a fellow, would care enough about him to learn whatever she had to learn to please him. And I'm afraid, dear, that your lovely brown eyes weren't nearly as sad as the tone you used to utter the melancholy words."

"Who could it be?" Maverick asked, chuckling.

"I wouldn't know, of course. But I imagine that in the fullness of time I'll find out. I imagine that he's poor, a city fellow. You'd not keep him to yourself, I suspect, if he had money and were a rancher."

Maverick stopped chuckling. She gave Opal a sidelong glance of appraisal. "How do you learn to think that way?" she asked.

"Be born poor, work to acquire your education, work for your bread. You quickly learn

"Like to like," Opal said easily, and they rode on to complete her inspection of the Diamond B-P.

Chapter 10

Toward the end of May it began to occur to Mike Lane that a certain door had been closed firmly against him. He was in the Business Men's Club, eating a lonely lunch, when big Bert Nutting strode into the handsomely paneled dining room. He called out to Bert, who gave him an affable nod and joined him at the table. "My treat," Mike said. "I owe you a lot, Bert, and don't ever think I forget it."

"One hand washes the other," Bert dismissed it. "How are things?"

"Fine," Mike said. "There's a good chance I'll pick up some business from Prather. This experimentation he's been doing with grass is leading him to develop another sideline. The old story, I guess, of the rich becoming richer. He thinks he ought to market grass seed, and I think I can help him in that little endeavor."

"Ought to be money in it," Bert opined. "A lot of worn-out land could be salvaged if grass were planted and water resources developed, conserved, used intelligently. There's a man named Charles Pettit over near Walnut Springs who's certainly proved that. He got together some seventeen thousand acres of loused up farms and pastures and woodlands and then he went to work. His place is a showplace now."

"Could be. One reason Prather is rich is that he doesn't think he knows everything. Show him a better way to do something, and he'll do it that way."

Bert ordered his lunch: roast beef, oven-roasted potato, split peas, coffee, apple pie. Mike listened, aghast. With the temperature well above a hundred degrees outside, he thought Bert's food intake was just about suicidal. He said so. The big, good-looking editor grinned lazily but didn't cancel the order. "I'll tell you

about food," he said. "You never really appre-
ciate food until you've sat in a foxhole three
days with nothing but K rations between you and
starvation. Made a little pledge there, Mike.
Pledged I'd eat three full meals a day the rest
of my life."

"Must have been rough," Mike said.

"Rougher, chum, than you'll ever know. That
was a nasty little war."

Mike had to admire the big fellow. After he'd
come home from that war, still uneducated and
poor, Bert had gotten his education under the
G.I. Bill of Rights and drawn dead aim on the
job he now had. To qualify for that job, Bert
had by sheer industry made himself a top writer,
a walking encyclopedia on the county, a gifted
after-dinner speaker, and the confidant of just
about every human being within the Tincup
area. When Mulrooney had retired, Bert had
been given the big boost because he was easily
the best qualified candidate. Yet Bert never gave
himself airs, was still the fellow he'd been before
success came to him.

"How's your business?" Mike asked. "I've heard chatter Agnew is thinking of establishing a rival paper in town."

"Heard that myself," Bert said. "More power to him. I don't approve of one-newspaper towns. You need to read and study conflicting opinions before you can hope to keep informed. More than chatter, by the way. As I understand it, Agnew is trying to get Prather and a few others to go in with him. They'd buy up the defunct *Herald* from Mrs. Littlefield, meaning they'd get the old plant and the wire services. Costs money, though, to start a paper these days."

"Losses could be written off tax reports."

"Sure. Still, the losses are real and somebody has to carry them. I understand, by the way, why Agnew soured on Opal. Crafty fellow. Always grabs opportunity by the throat. Our goof on that dog matter made us sitting ducks for him. But Opal got the full story to us just in time to prevent me from compounding the first goof with a fatal goof. Had the scorcher I'd written about his protests and threats appeared—well, he'd have had us dead. As it was, our retraction story the next day proved we had taken his protests seriously and wanted to make amends. End of an excuse to sue us, break us."

"Opal used her head on that one."

"Opal always uses her head," Bert said flatly. His meaning was crystal clear.

Mike returned to his office in a thoughtful frame of mind. He found Kitty typing the monthly report to Agnew, and he found Opal's successor toiling away on some little publicity squib calculated to win Mrs. Wentworth a few lines of praise in some nationally syndicated newspaper column. Ann Addie glanced up and said politely: "Did you want something, sir? I can always return to this. I think I have it now."

Mike smiled and took the chair beside her desk. He glanced at the talisman roses in the vase atop the file cabinet. "Nice flowers," he said. "I like the changes you've made in this office. No money or effort expended on appearance is wasted in this busines. How do you like Tincup?"

"Very much, sir," she said promptly. "I was

quite surprised to learn how busy and important it is. Stuck off here in this lonely corner of Texas, you almost forget it is a part of Texas. Yet its oil and its cattle and its horses and its hay—well, they add up to huge business, don't they?"

"The time will come, Ann, when Tincup will rank among the most important cities of Texas. We have a good administration here, a progressive bunch determined to see this city develop into a beautiful, well-rounded community. I think that anyone who remains in Tincup will have a good opportunity to grow with the city. I think that so sincerely I've invested all I own in this business and have turned down some rather good offers from some darned big corporations."

"So Mr. Agnew was telling me yesterday evening at his home, sir."

Mike's hand went on the alert. "Really? I didn't know you knew him that well."

"That was his point, Mr. Lane. He said he thought we ought to become better acquainted with one another so that I wouldn't repeat the blunders of my predecessor."

"Did he name those blunders?"

Ann Addie nodded, a fetching sight in a well-tailored green cotton dress. She had auburn hair and hazel eyes and a rather sassy scrap of nose, complete with freckles, that Mike intended to kiss one day. "Impulsiveness, arrogance, smug morality, to name just a few he mentioned."

"And did you assure him," Mike asked, "that you would never allow your morality to prevent him from making a fast and shady dollar?"

"I told him, sir, that I would always follow your orders, and that your orders are for me to conduct his affairs as he wants them conducted."

"Yours not to reason why, eh?"

"I'm practical," she said softly. "If I hire out, am paid the wages I ask, I do the work I'm ordered to do."

"Good," Mike said. "But in all fairness to Opal Bondy, I think you should be told she did an excellent job here. Despite his gripes, and I've heard him utter plenty, Agnew always insisted she handle his affairs."

"Yes, sir."

"Actually," Mike went on, "you steer a tricky course in this business. You must give your client much, no doubt of that, but you must never give him so much that you injure yourself in the process. After all, while clients come and go, the firm remains. And what do we market except a certain ability, a few good connections, a certain integrity? Catch?"

It was obvious she didn't understand. Mike therefore brought it down to concrete matters.

"For example," he elaborated, "Anew has the reputation of being a grabber. He'll grab anything that isn't nailed down, and he won't be a jot embarrassed if you catch him grabbing someone else's property. Well, we must always be careful not to become a party to that grabbing. For if we were careless, he would get the loot and we would get the dirty name. Our good connections would dry up; people would laugh if you mentioned us and integrity in the same breath."

"But how would it be possible for this firm to become involved in anything like that?"

Mike shrugged. "Well," he said, "Opal did some snooping one day and managed to prevent some costly unpleasantness for the *Informer*. Had her morality been more flexible, Agnew might now be cracking the whip at the *Informer*."

"Yet we're employed to forward his interests, sir."

"So much we do, but no more."

She smiled. Mike had a hunch he ought to ask why. He did ask. Her smile broadened. "Well," she answered, "I was just trying to relate this picture of the fair and square Miss Bondy to some gossip I overheard at the beauty parlor the other morning. If the gossip is to be believed, Miss Bondy is making the most of her opportunities at the Diamond B-P. They say that she's actually going into business with Mr. Craithorne and Miss Prather."

Mike was shocked. "That's fantastic!"

The hazel eyes regarded him a few moments, and then Ann Addie said: "I told Miss Prather as much, sir, when she telephoned a few minutes ago."

Mike grunted.

"Sometimes," Ann Addie said, "an assistant can assist in many ways, sir, assuming that it is to her financial benefit to do so. For example, sir, I suggested to Miss Prather that it might be well for her to make her telephone calls during Kitty's lunch hour. I said that sooner or later Kitty would recognize her voice."

"How did you recognize it?"

Ann Addie reached for a cigarette. She lighted it, inhaled, blew a smoke ring toward the window.

Mike got the point. He asked a bit wearily: "And in what other ways can you assist me, Ann?"

"By telling you you're a fool, sir. It's apparent, you see, that my predecessor is very much on your mind."

"But if one has a million, and the other hasn't?"

Ann Addie shrugged and blew another smoke ring.

Chapter 11

Much to Opal's delight, Mike Lane and his new assistant paid a surprise visit to the ranch just after dinner on June the fourth. The door-bell was rung, she opened it, and there the charmer stood, spruced as for an occasion of state. She kissed him. She couldn't help it. And having done so once, she proceeded to do so again. By that time the Prathers were in the hall and Mr. Prather was saying to his daughter: "In other words, pet, do as the lady *says*, not as she *does*.'

Opal drew back, blushing. "Well," she said defensively, "a friend is a friend, they say."

Mike suavely introduced his new assistant. He

stated he had come on important business and
he asked if he might have a few words with Maverick in private. The brunette beauty said very
icily that she knew of no business she wished to
discuss with him, but Mike said it was related to
her horse-riding venture, and finally Maverick
led him across the lawn to the small office building.

Opal took the new assistant in tow while Mr.
Prather ambled out for his customary after-dinner stroll to the distant bunkhouse area. "I understand you're doing fine," she told Ann Addie.
"The report came from Bert Nutting, no less, a
very difficult character to please."

"Really?"

"I quote. Opal, old girl, this Ann Addie has
you whupped to a frazzle. That girl is a born publicist. Give her three years here, a few bucks, and
she'll have the biggest and best agency in town.
I unquote."

"And here I've been worried about my job,
Miss Bondy."

"Call me Opal, Ann. Girl to girl, how do you

like Agnew?"

"Ugh."

"But interesting and challenging, Ann. That man can give you more problems in a day than most clients can in a year. Interesting problems, because they'd so darned unusual and different."

She led the girl along the hall to her bed-sitting room. She rang for Shorty, and when the old geezer had limped in complainingly, she suggested that coffee might please her guest. Shorty looked dubious. "Don't seem strong enough to drink my coffee, you ask me."

But he fetched it, and Ann sipped it and pronounced it good. After the beaming Shorty had left, Ann said lightly: "Actually, Miss Bondy, my presence here isn't accidental. Mr. Lane imagines I came simply because I was curious to meet you and see the Diamond B-P. I allowed him to think that because I'm not here on strictly agency business. All right?"

Opal shrugged. "Why not? I owe Mike nothing except a real slap one of these days. Shoot the works."

"Mr. Agnew would like a chat with you at any time you care to state."

"Really?"

"Mr. Agnew has always thought very highly of you, Miss Bondy. He told me to be certain to tell you so."

Opal nodded. "In other words, he's up to something dirty and needs the help of the talented stupid. What's it about, do you know?"

"A newspaper, Miss Bondy. Mr. Agnew, along with Mr. Prather and a few other wealthy men, is involved in trying to bring the old *Tincup Herald* back to life."

"Ridiculous! Might've done it successfully before Bert took over from poor tired Mr. Mulrooney. But not now. Bert would make mincemeat of them."

"Still," Ann said, "that's their intention, and they have the money. And Mr. Agnew would like to discuss some business with you."

Opal smiled. It gave her much pleasure to say: "Not interested, Ann. Will you tell him so?" Then, hearing Mike outside, she led the new assistant back to the great, plainly furnished living room. She found Mike looking flushed and angry, as if his discussion with Maverick had been stormy. She cocked an eyebrow at him, and he shrugged. "You can't ever do business with someone who has a million bucks; profitable business, that it. It has to be on their terms or not at all. May I talk to you privately, Opal? It won't take long."

Ann quickly said: "I'll just step outdoors and look around, if I may." Ann closed the front door very loudly behind her.

"What was the idea?" Mike raged. "Whatever we had you killed when you wouldn't cooperate! I won't be pawed over by anyone, you least of all!"

"Miss me, Mike?"

The raillery of her blue eyes was as effective as always. He had to wag his head sheepishly and say: "Well, maybe a little bit." But this, he would have her know, was something else again. The next time she saw him she ought to try to behave.

"Well," Opal said, "I was trying to set Maverick a good example. Mike, it's the saddest thing! That girl is hopelessly in love with Tate Craithorne and hasn't the least notion of how to behave. When Tate's here, she's as prickly as any cactus. A little warmth, a little natural behavior, and Tate would be roped and branded."

"Who wants a lunkhead for a husband? If it weren't for his family, he'd starve to death."

"But there is that money, you see. And there's much to be said for Tate. The other afternoon I had to return a few books Maverick borrowed from his library. I found him in the music room, playing something by Debussy. How beautifully he plays! Yes, and talks, Mike. We sat talking a long time, hours at least, and I wasn't once bored."

"Funny that a fellow like that should be going into the horse-raising business with Maverick."

"My idea. We were all out there one day, and Maverick was complaining about her workload. I said that if she had a few interested partners she could expand the business and still have a lighter workload. A couple of days later she told me to sell Tate. Told me she'd give me a small share of the business if I were successful."

"And you were successful?"

Opal smiled, remembering the triumph. . . .

Mike scowled, disturbed by her long silence. "Oh, you were successful, all right," he said, answering his own question. "You're all but strutting in that chair."

"I wanted to be successful. I like Maverick. I wanted her to have something really important and worthwhile to work at. You know, very often the difference between a child-woman and a woman is the difference between rejecting or assuming responsibility. I have a notion that if the business works out—"

"I could use that account, Opal. I know these Prathers. Once they get their teeth into something, they move. I want to move as this new business moves."

"Maverick said no?"

"Our five-minute chat consisted of a five-minute lecture on the nerve I had to bring Ann Addie here. It seems that Maverick has gotten the notion I dumped you, left you with no choice but to accept this job."

"You and Mr. Agnew," Opal said composedly. "I suppose I may forgive him now, however. A man who wants to publish a newspaper and who wants a silent partner such as Mr. Prather can be forgiven for wanting to please Mr. Prather."

The black eyes narrowed. "Who told you about that?"

"The wind blowing through the grass, of course. But what was your reward to be, Mike? Are you dreaming of becoming advertising manager of the new paper?"

"Don't be silly. My motive is what I told you it is. I thought Prather would throw me some business. And I still say I didn't dump you."

"May I come back, then?"

"Will you be reasonable?"

The door opened, and Mr. Prather returned from his stroll. He gave them an affable nod and looked around for the others. "Nice evening," he said. "Why don't you invite your friends to stay the night, Opal? You could take them on a fine moonlight ride."

"Business," Mike said shortly. "And speaking of business, sir, I just happened to bring some ideas I've worked out for making the trade more aware of your experiments here with various grasses. Mind if I leave the stuff for you to look over?"

The cattle baron shrugged. "As you wish," he said easily, "but I thought I'd give Opal that trade if she wants it."

Chapter 12

Maverick said: "The polecat!" Maverick switched her boot with her quirt and said: "A polecat like that ought to be staked in the Badlands to die of thirst!" She strode about the stable yard intensely, her glorious brown eyes blazing. "Did you cut him down?" she asked. "This civilized lady stuff is all right, maybe, but sometimes it's better to cut them down."

"As a matter of fact," Opal informed her, "we had a quite pleasant chat. I thought Ann was nice, didn't you?"

"He deserves her, Opal. Two of a kind. They

deserve each other."

"May I ask a question?"

"Shoot."

"Why are you so upset? I'm sure he didn't come here to flaunt her in my face. But even if he did, he was trying to trouble me, not you."

"Well, we're partners, aren't we?"

"Still . . ."

"And he said a few things you didn't hear, about Tate. If he hadn't been a friend of yours—"

"I know," said Opal. "I should be intelligent. I should see him as you do, as a hard-driving, me-first businessman who'd stomp anyone and everyone between him and a new account. But there's another Mike Lane. When you get to that fellow, you get to a glorious hero."

"If there's one thing I can't stand," Maverick yelled hoarsely, "it's slush! You coming with me or aren't you?"

Opal went with her, but regretted having done so a couple of hours later. When they reached the Prather-Craithorne Company, Maverick insisted that the time had come for her very junior partner to have a livelier mount. "An old plow horse like Daisy," she said, "doesn't glorify this operation. What would folks think if they knew you could have your pick of those Arabians but still rode Daisy?"

"She's fat and sweet-tempered and we understand one another. I love her. I won't betray her."

"Scared, Opal?"

"Scared?"

"Some of the hands think so. We got to jawing the other afternoon, and one said you were scared, and the others said you couldn't be paid to mount a real horse."

Opal looked into herself and chuckled. "Well, I dare say they're right. I suppose I should be ashamed—a Texas gal, no less."

"You know how to get over it?"

"How?"

"By climbing onto a lively horse and having it out with him. Could be, I suppose, it's the same with fancy parties. If you give one, the idea of giving them doesn't throw you any more."

Opal met her glance. Some quality deep in the

girl's brown eyes troubled her. She had the strangest notion suddenly that she was being maneuvered very skillfully by this range-bred girl in the dusty clothes.

"Go ahead," she said quietly. "You're cooking up a deal of some sort."

"Maybe we both should stop being afraid, Opal. Maybe I should give that fancy ball and invite the Craithornes, and maybe you should ride a real horse."

"You should give the ball, of course. You should know more people, people your own age, people who don't have to humor you to keep a job."

"Sure. Do I do as you say or do I do as you do?"

The challenge was unmistakable. The need to accept the challenge was equally clear. If she'd learned anything about Maverick during the weeks she'd spent on the Diamond B-P, Opal thought, it was that the girl put a very high value on physical courage. Maverick might like you, weakling though you were, but she'd never respect you until you proved you were as courageous as she.

Opal made a snap decision. "Bring the brute on," she said. "But I hope your fancy ball will be more successful than my riding."

Maverick gave an excited whoop and galloped on ahead. When Opal reached the big white barn, Maverick was leading out a horse almost as big as King. The horse looked all nerves, prancing and tossing his head and fighting the halter and lead strap. A couple of the hands heard the commotion and came running, the young redheaded cowpoke named Ted Thompson among them. Ted called: "Real edgy, that mount, Miss Prather."

Maverick yelled hotly for him to shut up. The savagery of her face was so shocking, he did shut up. He and the others backed off to a fence and perched atop it and watched while Maverick had the saddle put on and cinched tight.

At that moment, Opal suddenly wondered what in the world she was doing there and why she should risk her neck to please this girl. As

Maverick called for her to mount, Opal almost
turned to flee. But those bright, rather strange-
looking brown eyes wouldn't allow her to flee.
"It's a deal?" she asked. And after Maverick had
nodded, Opal got down from Daisy, pulled her
hat down tighter on her head, gave the Arabian
a dubious look and climbed aboard.

Maverick screeched.

The Arabian leaped as if terrified, and having
started to leap he never stopped. He climbed
straight for the clouds, he sunfished, he climbed
again. After the third leap he was screaming, a
mighty raging beast Opal couldn't control for the
life of her. The third jar of all fours on earth tore
a stirrup loose from her boot. She almost went
off. As the big head swung around, trying to bite,
she lashed out with her quirt and kept lashing
out, her blood running cold. Up he went again,
and down. Her body began to ache. A great blur
formed before her vision and remained there.

"Ride 'im, cowboy!" Maverick whooped.

And then it was over. A leap and a wriggle
cost Opal the other stirrup, and she wobbled on

the saddle. In that instant, the redheaded cowboy came riding across the corral, smashed down the big head, grabbed the bridle, fought the Arabian to a standstill. "Get off," he snapped. "Get off this bronc, Miss Bondy."

Opal got off, and her legs crumpled. Bruised, dizzy, every bone aching, she sat there sucking in air while the men came hustling over. "Li'l lady," one called, "you sure rode 'im! Ain't never been rode, but you stuck. Hey there, li'l lady, you let me wipe that blood from you."

Opal barely felt the hands working on her face. Suddenly, in the reaction to the fear and the punishment, she felt sick enough to vomit. She looked around in a panic for Maverick, but the girl was following Ted and the Arabian over toward the barn. Maverick was yelling up a storm and gesticulating violently.

Then a queer thing happened. Without warning, she floated off into a kind of stupor. She knew she was being taken back to the house and that Maverick was with her at last and that a doctor came and looked at her and said that she was

just bruised and stunned but that she'd live. But
that was about all she knew. She had no sensa-
tions of any kind, not even of the nausea that had
bothered her. At some time or other she must
have drifted off to sleep, for when she next became aware the world was dark beyond her window and a table lamp was glowing at the sitting
room end of her bed. She grinned, thinking that
Shorty was the strangest-looking nurse she'd ever
seen. "Hey," she joshed, "wake up. Don't they
shoot you for sleeping on duty?"

"Reading," he said. "Words kind of swum before me, so I was just resting my eyes. How you
feeling, girl?"

"Fine."

"That's the drug they give you. This doctor fellow stuck a needle in your arm and filled you up
with a drug. Wouldn't let 'em do that to me if
they paid me."

"I'm thirsty."

He got her water. He leaned over the bed and
crooned very paternally: "Now don't go makin' a
hog of yourself. Females, haven't got much sense.

Good for some things, maybe, but not for using their thinkers. You get too much water in you, it'll turn into bile an' make you puke."

"Shorty, how vulgar!"

"Sorry, Boss. Keep forgetting we got a female lady around. Now Maverick, she don't mind calling a spade a spade."

"Where is she, by the way?"

"Still in town, I guess. What happened is, a cowpoke made a mistake. You got the wrong horse. That horse you got, he's for rodeo riding. Big and strong and tricky. Fellows say you'd have gone down on the next jump."

"You're telling me!"

"You was riding in a rodeo, they'd have blowed the horn. Grabbed leather, you did, the first jump."

"You bet I did! That horse wanted to kill me!"

"Anyway," Shorty said, "Maverick skinned that Ted Thompson a dozen different ways, and then she fired him and drove him to town. If she'd had a gun with her, guess she would've plugged him."

Some of it came back, particularly a memory of the cowpoke running up to tell Maverick the horse was real edgy. Maverick had been furious with him and had told him to shut up. Meaning, of course . . .

Opal sighed. It was an effort, but she finally got to a sitting posture. Shorty put something or other around her shoulders and said very solicitously that she mustn't tucker herself out. Anger got the better of her. "Stop it," she said. "I was bruised and shaken and that's all. Why does Maverick hate me?"

"Huh?"

"Shorty, she knew all about that horse. Ted even warned her, and she told him to shut up." His eyes bugged. He turned and went back to his chair and sat down stiffly.

Suddenly her anger died.

"Kid stuff," Opal dismissed it. "We've been getting along fine, so why would she want to murder me?"

Shorty said nothing.

Opal thrust it from her mind. She was half dozing when Maverick came in much later to see how she was. Dressed in a tan suit, smiling, Maverick soon put things right again. "Changed my mind about firing Ted," she announced. "The boys had the wrong idea. We do a lot of hazing, and I guess Ted thought I wanted to trick you or something. Glad he took things into his own hands, though. You could have been killed."

"I was very happy to see him ride up, believe me."

"We'll try again tomorrow. I'll chose the mount myself."

"Nope."

"Honey, you *have* to! If you don't try again the moment you can, you never will ride other than a Daisy."

"Daisy's my speed."

"Well, we'll see. Mike Lane sent you his best. Happened to see him near the hotel."

"Did you kiss him for me?"

Maverick Prather actually turned ashen. She asked very hoarsely: "Did I *what*?"

"Mike does love his kisses, I'm afraid. By the way, you might invite him to that ball you'll be giving. Fine dancer and lots of fun, Mike Lane."

"Am I giving a ball?"

"That was the deal."

"Yes, but look what happened when you tried something you couldn't handle."

"But I did try, Maverick."

"And if I say no?"

The girl grimaced.

"Is it possible," Opal asked, "that you really don't care about Tate, or pleasing his parents?"

"I've told you that before, haven't I?"

"Who is it then? It has to be someone, Maverick. I'll tell you why. Every so often, just like that, you betray that there is someone. For instance, I heard you calling someone sweetheart the other day. I happened to step into the office building while you were on the telephone."

"Spy!"

"I'd like to help."

"Do you know what you're saying? Are you still woozy? Do you have the least idea of what you're saying?"

But there was no time for an answer then. Abruptly, without the least warning, Miss Maverick Prather burst into tears.

Chapter 13

There was a party, if not a ball. Bruce Prather took the position that the word of his daughter had to be honored. "No place on my ranch," he said very bluntly, "for a liar or a cheat." But the party, held on July fourth, was a fiasco. Half the invited guests just didn't bother to show up. The Craithornes, while they did come, made it quite apparent that they were really humoring the father, not the daughter. Tate was moody from beginning to end, Jeb Agnew bored everyone bragging of his business successes, and Mike, the scoundrel, spent most of his time chattering with Maverick. When the last guest had left, Shorty summed up the affair in the kitchen. "Funeral," he said, "would've been more fun."

Opal shushed him imperiously. After she'd dried the dishes and helped put them away, she went across the lawn to the office building. She found the air-conditioning system on and Mr. Prather sitting shirtless at his desk, a big cigar in his mouth. He arched his brows. "Do I bother you?" he asked. "Man has to have a place to cool off, to let off steam."

"I've seen undershirts before, sir. Never forget that I have an uninhibited father."

"In that case, have a chair. Want a cigar?"

She chuckled. She took the indicated chair and lolled back comfortably and luxuriated in the delicious coolness flowing from the vents high on the walls. Knowing him rather well now, she just sat there quietly to give him time in which to put two and two together. His: "Well, Opal?" when it came, told her he'd accomplished the addition.

"They won't change their minds, sir," she told him. "And if I were Maverick, to be honest, I'd not want them as in-laws. You know that, too. In fact, I think you've always known they won't change their minds."

"Did I now?"

"Also, Mr. Prather, you're not the type of man who'd want them in your family. They're so impossibly snobbish, affected."

"Girl has to marry."

"Why not the fellow she loves, sir? You know she loves someone else, and I suspect you know the fellow's name."

His eyes slitted. He carefully knocked ash from his cigar. "It seems to me," he said, "that you know a great deal, Opal, or think you do."

"I hit it last month, sir. I stepped in here, overheard a conversation. Then, the evening after my jolting, sir, I popped a question at Maverick and everything fell into place. It's someone else. You disapprove of him. You thought an experienced public relations expert could help. You hired me."

"Oh?"

"Which was foolish, Mr. Prather. I wonder why you and Mr. Agnew have the idea a public relations expert is a mind-reader. Certainly some objectives are rather obvious, but far from all. What was your point in bringing me here; what job did you really want me to work at?"

"What you're doing. Company for Maverick seeing that this home is more homelike. Take grass, Opal. This type requires this kind of soil and irrigation; another type requires something different. If you want to grow one kind of grass, you suit it to the terrain and the water conditions or you suit the terrain and the water conditions to it."

"Environment, then? You pay me seven hundred and found every month merely to create a proper environment for Maverick?"

"Maybe so."

"No, sir."

"In my next life," he said, "I won't allow a positive woman within a hundred miles of me."

Again Opal sat quietly, giving him time in which to think. Through the night came the sounds of a restless herd somewhere off in the east. She recalled that some two or three thousand head were being assembled in the shipping corrals along the railroad tracks. A huge order, Maverick had told her, and a good thing, too, because many of the steers would soon be too costly to keep. Maverick had invited her to watch the proceedings and had herself ridden off the moment the last guest had left. But who wanted to see hordes of confused, disturbed animals milling about inside shipping corrals?

"I think you're having a good effect on Maverick," Bruce Prather said. "You wouldn't notice that, of course, not knowing how she behaved before you arrived. All right. Let me say this. When your wild and woolly daughter suddenly starts paying attention to her hair, when she allows her nails to grow and manicures them properly, when she bakes her father a cake, when she suddenly takes an interest in growing flowers and fixing up the house . . . well, all that tells me I'm getting everything I hoped for when I hired you. But take it beyond that. Another thing you didn't know is that Maverick was sneaking off to meet this particular fellow. And that's stopped. I have my ways of getting information, so I know it's stopped."

"She called me a spy. Is that why?"

"But if you want this fellow's name," Bruce Prather said, "I'll give it to you. Mike Lane."

She drew a deep breath.

He nodded, smiling at her a bit sadly, a bit pityingly. "Sure," he said. "Now everything makes sense to you, doesn't it? Why it had to be you here, not anyone else. Why Agnew pressured folks into not hiring you, why I came riding to the rescue like a great big noble son of the Old West. Why Maverick fought to prevent me from hiring you—you understand that, too. And that horse you rode by mistake, you understand why the mistake was made?"

Again Opal drew a deep breath.

He leaned forward and stubbed out his cigar. "Miss Bondy," he said, "you might as well know something about me here and now. If Maverick is tough, it's because I'm tough. If Maverick is tricky and dirty, it's because I am. I know only one way to play my hand, and that's for keeps. And I'll tell you why. Because you don't pick up miles of Texas range and become a cattle baron by being a nice fellow. Some of this land I bought. Some I took. All legal, sure, but I took it, and if you don't think so, just notice you never see me in the Badlands where some of the former owners now live. So when you criticize Maverick, include me, and when you condemn Maverick, include me."

Opal forced herself to say calmly: "Well, of course I did both a long time ago, sir. People are made to be what they are. You raised her; naturally you had to be blamed for the mess she is."

"So here we are," he said flatly. "And I still say I got all I hoped for from you, and whether you like us or don't, I still want you to stay."

"Until I'm eliminated by some unfortunate accident, Mr. Prather?"

"There won't be any more accidents. What really happened is that she hoped to scare you off. But you never caught on, so you didn't scare."

"I caught on, but didn't have sense enough to realize it. Such a dear child!"

"If you want more money, I'll give you a thousand a month. If you want a future after you're finished here, I'll give you a contract to plan my grass-seed publicity for me. Yes, and to handle it, too."

"Does Mike know you know?"

"I don't think so. I throw him just enough business to let him think he has it his way."

"Maverick?"

"She knows I know something. Stands to reason. This fooling around with Tate is to keep me uncertain."

"Lovely situation, sir, isn't it?"

"Or we could handle it another way. I could let it be known you'll handle all my publicity. Maybe Lane would remember you're supposed to be his girl. And if you married Lane, I could toss the contract to your firm."

It baffled Opal. She said so. "Mr. Prather," she said, "it puzzles me every time you suggest you must do all these drastic things to keep Mike from marrying your daughter. But Mike is ten times the person your daughter is. Why do you imagine Maverick is worthy of Mike?"

Score one for Miss Bondy!

When his sputtering stopped, when he could speak fairly coherently, he said: "Well, I guess you'd better leave. Maybe you've done enough as it is. I think that Maverick, in her odd sort of way, sort of likes you. And maybe when she knows that I know and you know about Mike, well, we'll see. Why not leave now? I'll give you a check until the end of the month."

"Yup."

Score two for Miss Bondy!

"Listen," he growled, "don't use that tone with me, young lady. I'm a father doing the best he can for his only daughter. You haven't been hurt. You've made good wages and you'll get a good recommendation. You don't have any complaints."

He was still rumbling along in that vein when Opal excused herself politely to go back to the house.

Shorty had the vacuum cleaner going in the living room. He turned off the machine long enough to say very bitterly: "You an' your ideas that make work for an old man!" He restarted the machine, then noticed the gravity of her expression. "Hey," he assured her, "I was just talkin'. Can't a feller even talk?"

"I'll want the pickup truck in about an hour, Shorty. Can do?"

"This time of night? Where you goin'? Should think you'd wanna hit the sack."

"Quitting. Put m'roll behind my saddle pardner; I'm moseying on."

He laughed as he always did when she swaggered about in that cute way of hers and used Western lingo. He limped along behind her to her bed-sitting room. "How come you quit?" he wanted to know. "Ain't a bad outfit, this here Diamond B-P. Been with Mr. Prather a long time. Good chuck, good dinero, good treatment."

"Mission accomplished, Shorty. And you know how we Texans are: always restless for the next adventure. Scoot! I have things to do."

"Maverick sure won't like it."

At that particular moment, Opal didn't really

care a hoot. She said so and pushed Shorty out.
Alone, she didn't know whether to laugh or cry
or both. Glory, the poor disgusting fools! In the
end she did neither, because she heard a motor
turn over outside and developed a hunch that
Shorty was heading off in quest of Maverick. She
worked fast to get the necessary packing done and
some traveling clothes on. She lugged everything
outdoors, sat down on her largest suitcase and
waited. When the pickup came, Maverick at the
wheel, she matter-of-factly began to put her lug-
gage in the rear. Maverick climbed down, lifted
both brows, shoved her Stetson well back. "Nothing I can say to change it?" she asked.

"Nope."

"Anything I can square? All I know is that
you had a talk with Pop. You ought to know better than to let Pop get under your skin. If he said
something that hurt your feelings, I'm sorry."

"Wrong girl for the wrong job, Maverick,
that's all. Sorry I didn't know about you and
Mike sooner. Would've spared you a number of
fibs, your father money, me a lot of effort."

The beautiful brunette drew back a step. She reminded Opal once more of a glittering and dangerous blade, and knowing now from experience that the danger could be all too real, Opal slipped by her and got into the pickup. "Do you drive or does Shorty or do I?" she asked.

"Won't do you any good," Maverick said. "Now that it's out, I'm glad. No crime in loving a fellow; no crime in going after whatever you want. Didn't want to hurt you. You're okay, Opal; maybe too much of a sissy, but okay. You stuck on that bronc longer than I thought you would. Expected you to crawl, I don't know why."

Now, for the first time, Opal really became angry. She said with deceptive calm: "Oh, yes, that reminds me." She stepped down from the cab, hesitated, then unloosed a roundhouse slap that Maverick could easily have avoided had the girl not been too dumbfounded to move. The slap made a soul-satisfying sound to Opal in the July night. The girl's cry of pain, of outraged pride, was ample payment for a certain dirty trick.

But this was Maverick Prather, the badly

spoiled daughter of a cattle baron! So the girl had to cry out again, this time in pain and terror as quite competent hands found the judo grip they wanted and flipped her around and threw her. Grinning, quite pleased with herself, Opal then returned to the cab of the pickup. "It isn't civilized to brawl," she said gently. "But you must never confuse good manners or proper behavior for weakness, Maverick. And you must never underestimate a girl who's not had things handed to her all her life. Catch? If you don't, go ask your father."

Opal slid behind the steering wheel, started the truck and drove off.

Chapter 14

Playing her cards shrewdly, Opal treated her mother and herself to a leisurely vacation in Mexico. Her efforts to coax her father into accompanying them were completely unsuccessful. "Business before pleasure," he said, "and anyway, I got enough of Mexico during my drifting years. You kids go ahead and have a good time. I'll hold the fort." And if he thought the trip a childish attempt to buy time and to prove something to Mike Lane and a few others, he gave no sign. He waved them off on a humid morning, his last words being a command to drop him a card from time to time just to assure him they were still alive.

Opal's first thought was to make the grand loop trip that would carry them into Mexico by way of Laredo and back into the United States again by way of Nogales in Arizona. Her mother thought that was a nice idea, but changed her mind the first evening as they sat studying road maps in their motel room. "But that would be thousands of miles!" she cried. "I simply couldn't endure it!" They finally settled on an easy tour to Mexico City and a two-week stay in Guanajuato, a town Mrs. Bondy had heard much about from an uncle who'd worked for a mining company down there among the mountains. "They say," she argued, "that Guanajuato is among the most beautiful old towns on this continent. Anyway, who wants to go, go, go all the time?"

Mexico City was a horror of traffic that scared Opal out of a year's growth. On their first evening there, after a five-day trip across desert and mountains, she was almost hit three times by drivers who appeared to believe Avenida Juarez was a race track. She had the desk clerk at the Hotel

Regis arrange for her car to be garaged, and they did their sightseeing on foot, in buses or in cabs. But the trip north through the mountains to old Guanajuato was quite a different matter. Here the going was easy, the traffic problems nonexistent. They took two days, stopping wherever they wished to snap picture or tour markets or chat with likely-looking people not above conducting conversations in pidgin Spanish. In Guanajuato they found pleasant quarters at the Posada Santa Fe, and settled down to a peaceful existence of walking or eating or sleeping when they chose. An elderly Mexican gentleman looked upon Opal's mother and found her fair. He contrived to meet them. He invited himself to guide them about. He did guide them about. They visited mines and they visited cathedrals and they walked the hilly crooked streets and one day they climbed what seemed to be miles of steps built into a hillside to get a closeup look at the great statue of Pipila. That evening was crowned by an invitation to have dinner in the home of *Señor* Obregon's granddaughter. It was fun!

Theresa was a pepperpot of a girl possessed of a grand passion for her husband, her children, her table, and "the conversation." They ate and they played with the small fry, and then they went outdoors and discussed all sorts of things very earnestly and pleasurably under an enormous golden moon.

That night, walking home, Opal's mother made a decision. "Dearest," she said, "I hope you and your father will be quite happy alone together. I've just succumbed to the Obregons. Too bad, but I did tell your father he mustn't ever take me for granted."

"Poor old Pop!"

"Had enough? We won't have a pleasanter day than this has been. Vacations should always end on a supremely happy note."

"We could linger another month or so. So far, all we've spent is that loot I never did earn at the ranch in July. But I guess you're right. Now's a good time to leave."

In the morning they set off on the return trip to the States. Perhaps because they'd wired to expect them on August the twenty-seventh, they returned to an immaculate house, a well-groomed front lawn, and a man who didn't look as if he'd gone to seed at all. "Why didn't you stay longer?" they were teased. "Look, kids, I've got a poker game lined up for tonight, so why don't you head for the hotel?"

But after he'd had his fun and they'd chattered about the trip, he gave them a rundown on all that had happened since they'd left. First of all, he reported, Mr. Jeb Agnew had come to the house not once but four times to leave a message. The message was always the same. He hoped Opal would get in touch with him before she sought a job elsewhere.

At this point, Mr. Bondy shot Opal a puzzled glance. "Beats me," he said. "Two or ten times that fellow said you're good at your work. Never thought you were much good for anything, button."

"More," Opal demanded.

Well, Maverick Prather had driven over the day after they'd left, her right arm in a sling.

That girl had been a regular spitfire, yelling all sorts of threats and insults.

"Judo trick Bert taught me," Opal explained, anticipating the parental question. "No feeling of shame, either, sir. That girl almost killed me one day."

"Violence is always shameful," Mrs. Bondy said crisply. "*I'm* ashamed of you, really I am."

Then, Mr. Bondy reported, Mr. Prather had come calling and Mike Lane had come calling and Bert Nutting had come calling and Ann Addie had come calling. He got up and went to the desk over near the windows and came back with a little pile of messages. "What they all amount to," he said, giving them to her, "is that they want you to call or go see them the second you get back."

"And Tate Craithhorne, too?"

Mrs. Bondy stiffened. Opal went to the telephone and called Tate anyway. He was surprised to hear from her and obviously delighted by the news he was the first to be told she'd come home. "Dinner," he said, "Not here, although my parents approve of you. I want a private conversation with you. Will eightish be satisfactory?"

"Not this evening, Tate. I have to unwind. A long bath, a long sleep, then clothes to renovate. We've been living out of suitcases for more than a month."

"Eightish," he said. "Wear something simple, if you wish."

He actually hung up on her protests!

"Important fellow," she told her parents. "The voice of decision, of authority. Think you'll like having the Craithorne millions, decision and authority in the family?"

"Me," her father said, "I can get along with almost anyone."

Significantly, Mrs. Bondy said nothing.

It didn't matter to Opal, however. She was dressed in something simple at the appointed time and was waiting on the porch when Tate drove up in a red Jaguar convertible. She went back into the house and got a scarf and wound it about her hair. Tate said warmly: "Quite acceptable, Opal. You wear just about anything with distinction, did you know?"

"I didn't know."

"My mother thinks so. Indeed, my mother was much struck by you. She said you always comported yourself with the poise and correctitude of a lady."

"She's very kind, Tate."

"I think so. I'm aware, by the way, that many think I'm dominated by her. What people fail to understand is that I can discuss things with her. That's important in country such as this. No offense intended, but most of these ranchers and businessmen around here are oafs. They know cattle or business and the country, but little else. But there is much else, and all of it important. A phrase of music is eternal beauty; a well-written line delights man today and delights man a thousand years from today. I give you Plato or Homer as examples."

Opal settled back on the seat. Their destination was obviously out of town, because Tate was skirting the business section and aiming in the general direction of the highway. When they reached the highway he speeded up the pace, and the car surged along with delightful smoothness and authority.

'Before dinner," Tate said, "we must conclude our business. It's occurred to me that I can use your services at the house. My library is a hodge-podge that requires rearrangement, and the same might be said of the music and the museum. More, my mother does tend to become a bit lonely. So I thought that you might want to work for me."

"Nice of you, Tate. Jobs aren't always readily found in Tincup. But I ought to say that my assignment at the Diamond B-P was something I was more or less compelled to take. The whole thing was idiotic, too, the sort of thing only hard-headed businessmen would think up. They're so accustomed to buying this or that, having affairs proceed according to detailed plans, they forget some things can't be bought or made to proceed as they wish."

He smiled. "Oddly enough," he said, "it might have worked out precisely as Mr. Prather wished. Maverick and Mike haven't seen one another in weeks. Maverick was complaining to me about that."

"You knew, too?"

"Certainly. You see, I was as disinterested in Maverick as she was in me. But sometimes, Opal, when the mighty order a thing done, you can't say no quite as bluntly as you'd like."

"What would happen, Tate, if I did accept? Exit Maverick?"

"I would imagine so. I would imagine, too, that Mr. Prather would be annoyed. There might even be some unpleasantness. But if a man sees a rose, Opal, and he wishes to have that rose, does he permit its thorns to deter him from plucking the prize?"

Opal inhaled sharply.

"One dreams, one looks, and there the dream walks," Tate patted her hand, laughed and drove on.

Chapter 15

Within a week it was noticed, within a month there was gossip, and by the end of September there were fireworks. A grim Bruce Prather came to the house on Saturday afternoon and surprised Opal in the act of painting the window trim. "Let's powwow," he said. He took her arm forcefully and led her to the shade along the fence. He said bluntly: "I don't like what you're doing, Opal. I don't like the Prathers to be overlooked whenever the Craithornes give parties. I don't like seeing my daughter forced out of the herd and made into a loner. And I don't like two-bit help that gives itself airs. Understood?"

"You look thinner," she said. "Don't tell me

Shorty's gone back to the old chow!"

"I don't say you haven't a squawk coming. I don't say you have any reason to love Maverick or care a hoot about me or my plans. All I'm saying is there are some things I can't let you do."

"What am I doing?" Opal asked.

She puzzled him as she'd always puzzled his daughter. Bruce Prather fell back a step and took a good look at her. She wasn't particularly impressive at first glance. Her clothes were inexpensive, her hands were paint-smeared, her blue-black hair was every which way. She looked like just another girl to him, and not at all formidable. But when he looked more closely he saw a curious strength in that lovely face, particularly around the mouth and chin. More, the eyes that met his simply and unembarrassedly were the eyes of a person who knew precisely what she was doing, why she was doing it, and that she would go on doing it forever if she elected to.

"You're a strange one," he said. "I suppose I should have realized that straight off. Agnew doesn't make mistakes about people, and he was always impressed by you. And there's Maverick. You never had too much trouble handling her, either."

"Just a girl, sir, trying to go along through life as pleasantly as possible. Think of it this way. Back in April I was a girl with a job she liked and a fellow she loved. You and Mr. Agnew weren't content to leave me in peace. You felt you needed me; he felt he needed to please you. Neither you nor Mr. Agnew nor Mike Lane ever stopped to think I had a right to go on living the life I was leading. You wanted something, and you're a big man, accustomed to getting what you want. So to perdition with my interests, my desires! Lies to Mike and lies to me. The great man schemes and uses his weight, and lo, the great man triumphs! No concern to you, sir, if I lost the fellow I loved, and no concern to you, sir, if I died under the stomping hoofs of a wild beast! You want, you get. That's all that matters to you on earth; that's all you know on earth. Well, sir, exult in your triumph now!"

"It wasn't figured that way."

"How was it figured?"

"I told you. I thought with you right there, helping her, being her friend, Maverick would snap out of it. I thought that with you there, helping her, the Craithorne thing might work out. I don't go around scheming and using my weight, as you called it, to hurt deliberately a kid girl I don't even know."

Opal said nothing, supposing that to a degree he was being honest but that neither the honesty nor dishonesty mattered much now. She went back to the important thing.

"Mr. Prather," she drawled, "I hate to have to put it this way, but you don't scare me even a little bit. I'll do today and tomorrow and the next day whatever I wish to do, regardless of your approval. Mr. Prather, I have news for you. This is Texas, the chunk of land that became a state of the Union because its folks didn't like being pushed around. Anything else on your mind?"

Had she been a man, his fist would have shot out hard. His angry flush, his flaming brown eyes

told her so. Hoarsely, Bruce Prather asked:
"What are your terms, Opal?"

"For what?"

"You know."

"I don't know."

"What are your terms?"

"Everything in the open, Mr. Prather. That's
how it should have been in the first place."

"Talk up Maverick to Tate; turn the charm
loose on Lane. How much?"

"Nothing."

His eyes narrowed.

Opal laughed. "After all," she laughed, "why
shouldn't I marry the position and the dinero?
I'm much lovelier and brighter than poor Maverick."

Bruce Prather left muttering and fuming. . . .

On the other hand, Bert Nutting tried sweet
reason. He invited her for a talk when she telephoned him more news about the Craithornes to
print on the society page. The talk was held in his
office, with the door tightly closed and Bert smiling pityingly at her, as he might at a silly child.

"It won't work," the big guy predicted. "If I thought it would, that you'd be happy, I'd wish you luck and do my best to forget you. But you aren't that sort, sweetheart, and you know it."

"What sort am I?"

"Right now I don't know," he confessed. "You fool a fellow. You put on that sweet smile, that gentle expression comes into your eyes, and I suspect you're a very fine and wholesome sort. But if a person is the sort who can put on a smile and turn on the charm at will, to win a point, she can't be the girl I've always thought her to be."

"Maybe I'm not entirely nice or entirely evil, Bert. Could be, in fact, I'm an average person who can be sweet or unsweet as the need arises. Enough! The Craithornes have decided to share some of their treasures with the louts of this area. Tate screamed; I battled on. How can there be culture, I said, if the cultured don't instruct the uninformed? Great delight in the maternal breast, for there, with one shrewd stroke, is found an occupation for Tate and multitudinous huzzahs from the grateful populace."

Bert whistled, for this was indeed important news. He snatched the material she'd brought along and read it quickly, almost avidly. When he'd finished, he reached out and patted Opal's head. "All the nasty thoughts withdrawn, all the innuendoes retracted."

"Seemed a logical solution of Tate's problem and my problem. I ask you, Bert: am I the type that can inventory all those things and catalogue them and keep them in order? Nonsense. Pass the problem on to the city, say I. But you must always leave people a little better off than you found them. There's the secret of my profession. No matter what they want, whether it's their names in the paper or a letter of commendation from a wheel, you get them that and just a bit more, too. They say, then, that you have ability. They remember you. You get another job, and you grow. First thing you know, you have an agency, a successful business."

Opal paused, then dropped her little bombshell. "Which reminds me, Bert: I have another story here. Care to run the announcement for me for free? I'll cook you chicken stew with dumplings one of these days."

He read the story.

He nodded, for now it made sense to him, sense he didn't necessarily want to cheer over, but which he could accept more easily than he'd been accepting other things concerning her and her behavior. "The point?" he asked. "Quite clever, Opal."

"It came to me during my vacation in Mexico, Bert. I've been a dope. I've allowed Mike and Prather and Agnew to push me around. I didn't want to go out to that ranch, but I went. I didn't want to battle that pathetic girl out there, but I did. I didn't want to leave Mike, but I left. All for one reason, Bert. This live and let live philosophy can ruin you. So no more. Tate's all right. I understand him; he understands me. And now I'll have my own place, find my own customers, and achieve a position none of them can threaten or destroy. See?"

"When do you open your doors?"

"I have. Just now."

"Where?"

"Office in the lovely Craithorne home. Mrs. Craithorne is thrilled. She now has more in her life than she's had in years: the library-museum to fret about, my business to fret about. I like her. Found out she wasn't snobbish or affected at all; just a person having difficulty fitting her square self into a round hole. Fine for everyone."

"Want my business?"

Opal's blue eyes shone. "I might," she said, "even cook two chicken stews for an editor who gave me business like that."

"Knock out the *Herald*, then. There's the assignment."

"But I thought you approved of competition."

"Not that kind. Agnew will be Agnew until the day he drops. He'll sell sensation, not news. I know the character he plans to bring in to run the paper. To build circulation, they'll sling mud and take pot shots at the substantial folks in town, the folks who really built Tincup instead of exploiting it."

"For how much a week?" Opal asked. "I must be practical, you see."

"Two hundred a week, if you'll sign a contract for a year. Don't kid yourself; this will be a tough scrap. You'll have to tangle with Agnew, with Prather, a few other of those hard-driving boys; maybe even with Mike Lane."

She stood up, laughing. "Lovelier and lovelier, Bert."

"But don't marry a fellow you don't love," Bert said, getting back to the big thing. "You're not that desperate, you see."

Opal barely heard, for she was daydreaming a beautiful dream in which Mr. Agnew and Mr. Prather and Mr. Mike Lane were kneeling before her and asking her for her surrender terms. . . .

But when she saw the old scoundrel and told him her assignment, it didn't work out that way at all. "Foolish," he said. "Brains aren't enough. Lots of folks with brains around, more than mine, but they don't have my gushers and other stuff. Maybe take a little longer to break the *Informer*, but I'll break it."

"Why?" Opal asked.

He laughed. The hard blue eyes looked at her and through her. "Best way to control a town is to control its newspaper. What folks don't know can't hurt them."

"Can't be done here, sir."

"Can be; will be. You sign that contract yet?"

"No. The *Informer's* lawyer is drawing it up."

"Three hundred a week you want to work for me?"

"No."

"Four hundred?"

"No."

"Ann Addie gets kicked out, Mike Lane gets told off, Maverick Prather apologizes, Bruce Prather gives you some land and builds you a nice home."

"All for what, sir?"

"Why should I tell you?"

"Because I know where certain bodies might be buried, sir?"

His face went still as death.

"It's odd," Opal said. "I look back over all

these months and I'm stuck by one big fact. Almost all these complications began the day you came to my office with that picture of you kicking a poor dog. If I were a less trusting soul, Mr. Agnew, do you know what I would think? I would think you never were slashed by that dog, that you had the police put a lie on the record only when you saw a chance to sue the *Informer* and then take a chunk of stock as a settlement."

"You think funny things."

"Say you made a promise of big business to Mike if you heard I wasn't there any more. Say you met with Bruce Prather to convince him that I, a publicist, could do a job on Maverick only a trained psychiatrist can do."

"Go on."

"When did Ann Addie learn the truth, sir?"

"What's that?"

"She came to me with your proposition. That means you needed me, or thought you did, to handle her. Why else would you tell her of your newspaper plan?"

"Any other questions?"

"No, sir."

"What you don't understand," he said, "is that a feller like me always gets things his own way."

"It has to be something like that, though. How else explain the offer of income and other concessions amounting to about ten times what my work may actually be worth?"

At that point he howled threats at her like a coyote at bay.

Opal laughed at him. "Please," she said, "stop being so rude to a future Craithorne. Most unseemly, good sir."

Chapter 16

Mike Lane was sincerely shocked. "Brother," he snapped, "and to think she had me rolling hoops for her! It's what I've always said: Kiss 'em and leave 'em, and keep your illusions intact."

Bert Nutting looked around Mike's office. There were vases of flowers here and there, a couple of oil landscapes on the tan walls; a smell of newness exuded from the leather armchair in which he sat. He guessed that Mike had done fairly well that year. He had to admire the man. Only incessant plugging could explain the man's success in a town dominated by business corporations that had enormous publicity staffs of their own.

"Good luck to her," Mike said bitterly. "I say

good luck to her, Bert."

"Doesn't need luck, Mike. A couple of times this summer I thought she'd break her neck, but she always landed on her feet. There are some people like that. I recall a fellow in France during World War II. This fellow never missed a square meal throughout fifteen solid months of combat duty. No matter where we went, he found chow to make you drool. Once we had to scout some rugged terrain, and we ran into some rough opposition. Boy, we were pinned down, and I mean pinned. Along about chow time one of the fellows looked at this guy and told him to go ahead and find himself a real meal this time. So this guy goes over to a half smashed barn, and when he comes back he's all but bending under a side of smoked beef."

"Luck, that's all it is, just luck."

"Maybe not in Opal's case, though. There Tate was, and she saw him and realized the possibilities. Notice Maverick couldn't snatch him; notice you didn't snatch Maverick?"

"You think I was after Maverick?"

"Weren't you?"

"Listen. To me, all that girl was and is amounted to a cattle empire that needed my services. Sure, I played the old game. No denying that. Wrong? Maybe, but that's how the game is played, and you have to run before the wind. But get this and get it straight. I had her right in the palm of my hand, and I still have her there. If I wanted to marry her tomorrow I could marry her tomorrow."

"Why don't you?"

"And others," Mike said, "and I'm not bragging. You can kid me all you want, Bert, but it just so happens that when I call a woman beautiful I mean it, and that when I say I'm honored to be with this or that woman, I mean that, too. And women don't hate you for sincere emotion. They'd hate you if you played it small and mean, but I never have and never will."

"Why don't you, to repeat a good question?"

Mike looked down at his desk. Bert had come at a rotten time. Right there before him were papers which would give Bert and the *Informer* some very rugged moments in the months ahead. The prospectus, the staff, the policies, the advertisers already bound by contract—there it all was. Finish the work today, get the okay from Agnew and Prather tomorrow, and the *Herald* would rise from the grave to turn Tincup on its ear.

'I'm busy," Mike said. "Sorry to seem rude, Bert, but I do work sometimes."

"Old newspapermen can read type as easily upside down as right side up. The first few lines of that prospectus are interesting, Mike."

"Nothing personal, you understand. I was here all along to be hired if you wanted to stop Agnew."

"I'll bet on Opal Bondy, Mike. As I've said, she has talent for landing on her feet."

It scored big. In the mugginess of the October afternoon, with rain threatening to lash down at any minute, the face of Mike Lane went taut.

"Opal's bucking Agnew and Prather, you mean?"

"I mean just that."

"She's insane! They'll clobber her!"

"Have they yet?"

"The Craithornes may be strong, but—"

And then Mike got it, and he went limp behind the desk. . . .

Long after the smiling Bert had left, Mike gave the matter deep thought. It occurred to him that Opal was shooting the works, was running as wild as any maverick steer on the range, and the realization troubled him. With luck she might escape being clobbered, but she'd certainly not escape being hurt.

Mike grimaced. He then got up and went across the hall to Ann Addie's office. "Business calling," he said. "Wind up that *Herald* work on my desk will you?"

"Certainly, sir. Mr. Nutting has a booming voice, hasn't he? I suspect Miss Prather heard as much in the reception room as I heard here."

"Maverick?"

"Kitty told her you were busy and she agreed to wait."

Mike swallowed. He didn't want to ask the question, but had to. He croaked: "And what did *you* hear Ann?"

"That you could marry her tomorrow; that you were playing the old game. Need I go on, sir?"

Mike sank against the desk. He wagged his head weakly. "I talk too much," he muttered. "Bad habit, Ann."

"You know what, though, sir?"

"Well?"

"Some of it was very interesting. The declaration of sincerity, for instance, the statement you never have and never will play it small and mean. You haven't, sir."

"Oh?"

She laughed softly, pleasantly. "I was scared, I'll admit that now, sir, when I came here and heard some of the talk about you in town. I had visions of having to battle for my honor eight hours a day. But you were always so pleasant, so polite, so considerate, so helpful, I gradually forgot you're a wolf in man's clothing. When I heard that talk I found it difficult to believe you were talking about yourself. No offense intended, sir."

"But I am offended."

"Sure. But Kitty tells me she never had to come armed with a baseball bat, either, and we compared notes, as women will. What we've decided, sir, Kitty and I, is that you're a tolerable employer and that we're very happy to work for you. And I, sir, have decided more."

"Oh?"

"Why don't you marry her, Mr. Lane? She's quite a nice girl, it seems to me. Certainly you shouldn't fear her."

His mouth snapped shut.

"Also, sir, you don't need business of the type Mr. Agnew gives you. We have many worthwhile accounts and could take on more if we terminated our relationship with him."

"In this business you keep every account you can grab!"

"And so lose other accounts which might be more profitable and satisfactory? I'm unable to see the logic in that, sir."

"Yet you were all for helping Agnew, as I

recall."

"Yes, sir."

"What changed your mind-"

"Boy who had a dog. Pursuant to Mr. Agnew's instructions, sir, I bought a dog and then tracked down the boy who owned that dog that was killed last April. Interesting assignment. Private commission, by the way."

Mike's eyes rounded.

"Oh, the murdered dog, sir, did have teeth, so the police report of the slashing was believable. But no front teeth, sir, no fangs. Have you ever tried to slash someone with your back teeth? Quite an accomplishment, that."

Mike sat down on a corner of her desk. It flashed through his mind that Miss Ann Addie was quite a bright young woman of considerable initiative and ambition. Such a woman could be useful to a growing agency in a growing city such as Tincup.

He said at last: "Sort of sickens me, Ann. Maybe it didn't happen as we think, but the mere thought of it is rather sickening."

"A boy is an odd sort of creature, Mr. Lane. He burns for revenge. Or he burns, under the proper stimulation, to become a fierce defender and upholder of the law. We talked. We talked, if you will, in the Badlands. Such a dreary world up there, a world of bare rocks, of truncate cones that resemble extinct volcano cones. The mother served me tea, no less. We talked, as women will, of housekeeping and clothes and the need of the young for proper education. And at last, sir, I searched into my heart and found lodged therein one small shred of pity for a taker. I appointed the boy to be the taker. I entered into a pact with him. No shot in the dark, no violence of any kind, unimpeachable behavior in all other respects for three months, and I would find a decent position for the father and a decent home for the family."

"Quite a pact, Ann."

"You approve?" she inquired with elaborate casualness.

Her tone put him on guard.

"Well, of the general idea," he hedged, "but not, necessarily, of whatever arrangements you've made or intend to make."

"If I were given a raise, sir, I'd sink my savings into the down payment for a nice little ranch that's going begging. With the loot derived from the ranch, I could pay the father and house the family."

"For that raise, Ann, would you give Mr. Jeb Agnew the news we've just terminated our agreement?"

"For that raise, sir, I would tell the Devil himself he's a disgusting old goat."

"What raise were we discussing?"

"Say five dollars a week? That would convince me, sir, you intend to retain my services after your marriage to Miss Bondy."

"And if I don't marry her?"

"Why, fifty, sir, because I'd then know you couldn't replace me easily."

"Go see Agnew," he ordered, and walked out.

It was odd. By the time he'd reached the street Mike knew precisely what he had to do and why he had to do it. He drove directly to the bank. He withdrew a thousand dollars from his check-

ing account and got a fresh book of bank checks
for good measure. The teller asked: "Going to
Nevada or something for the roulette, Mike?"
Mike told him he wasn't that crazy and moved on.
His next stop was at Opal's home. He told Mrs.
Bondy that, crazy or not, he was going to marry
her daughter after all, and he ordered her to pack
clothes suitable for a honeymoon in Mexico. Mrs.
Bondy sat down, grinning from ear to ear. "Now
that's sweet," she said. "I always did want a boy,
you know. But I'm not sure I want such a master-
ful boy or such a reluctant boy. And there's one
little technicality, Mike. Forgive me for raising
it, but has my daughter been swept off her feet?
I expected, I don't know why, to have a million-
aire son-in-law."

"Ma, he wouldn't be fun."

"Don't you dare call me Ma, you!"

"All right, so I goofed. Kid stuff. Okay. But
don't you ever think for one instant that I have to
talk that daughter of yours into marrying me. All
I have to do, Ma, is snap my fingers and she'll
come running."

"If she does, Mike, so help me she'll have to baby-sit her own babies."

"Got the stuff packed yet, Ma?"

"Mike Lane!"

He strode to the door. "All right, just have it ready when we come by."

And on Mike continued to what he expected to be his last stop. It gave him a jolt to see the big, square, four-story white house in which Opal now worked and in which she could live as a Craithorne. He almost turned back. Who was he, what was he? But that cross-grain in his nature wouldn't permit him to take this no as final, either. He halted the shabby car and mounted the elegant steps and rattled the big brass knocker. When Tate Craithorne himself appeared, he shouldered the fellow aside and stepped into the main hall. "Opal ready?" he asked, deciding to give it to the guy hard and quick. "Heading for Mexico and marriage this afternoon."

Tate Craithorne said: "Nonsense." He then said testily: "I don't understand Opal. We have a full schedule of work, yet she wanders off, if you please, to explore the Badlands with Maverick. I thought they detested one another."

"Maverick Prather?"

"As for marrying her, old man, that may be. But definitely not today. First things first, and we do have work to accomplish."

A great roar stopped him, the roar of a badly frightened man. "You fool," Mike roared, "that Maverick plays for keeps!"

Tate would have argued it, but Mike left before he could begin.

Chapter 17

The women sat down on a flat-topped rock that commanded a fine view of some hundred square miles of Texas range. Even from this height, the Prather holdings dominated the scene. The irrigated sections formed rich green squares against the background of brush and scrubland. The various irrigation ditches and other waterways gleamed under the threatening sky. And there lay the adobe building, lair of the great cattle baron. Studying the building, Opal wondered why she'd ever been afraid to live in it or work for a Prather. The building looked quite insignificant, and so did the Prather beside her.

"Nice ride," Opal said politely. "It was nice of you to think of Daisy."

"Daisy missed you," Maverick said. "Never knew a plow horse could be that emotional."

"It's because Daisy and I have much in common. We both prefer to amble peacefully through life."

"You know what my father thinks?"

"What?"

"He thinks that's true. We talked about you the the other evening. He said he should never have angered you. He said that if he'd not angered you, your peace-loving disposition would have kept you on the ranch."

"And you said what, Maverick?"

"I said no. I said that when two cats want the same fish, they'll spit and claw sooner or later."

"The trouble is,'" Opal said, "that I sympathize with you. It would be easier if I didn't."

"Easier on which cat, Opal?"

"On me, of course. It's always much easier to help someone if you can be objective. Ah, well, what did you wish to discuss, and in what way do you think I can help? I like the idea of helping you to do something to help the people up here."

The brown eyes twinkled. "I could tell you something, Opal; something Pop told me a long time ago. It's to trust no one but yourself, and that only when you have one eye on your face in the mirror. Think you can find your way out of here alone?"

Opal looked down at her boots. She forced herself to say steadily: "I believe so."

"Care to bet, Opal?"

"I would be betting, wouldn't I?"

Maverick considered that. "Well," she conceded, "I guess you would be. It isn't that I care about Lane or Tate. You know that, I hope."

"Really?"

"You don't throw me the way you did on my place and get away with it. It's what my father always says. Give people an inch and they'll grab the range."

"Or if you can't win despite all the advantages of beauty and money, try the old sneak attack. Are you proud of yourself, Maverick?"

It almost worked. The girl jumped up as if to hurl herself forward. But she calmed down and even grinned. "It's the winning that counts, not how you win. Have a nice walk home, Opal. Just in case you do make it, I'll have some smart story to spin."

She walked over to King and climbed onto the the saddle. She clucked for Daisy to follow as she swung King around, but Daisy didn't follow. Big fat Daisy gave a look at Opal and remained put.

Maverick rode in on Daisy and grabbed for the bridle.

Daisy backed away.

Opal said gently: "The odd thing is, Maverick, that your idea of helping the folks up here would pay rather big dividends. Now consider Tate. Tate seems much happier now that he's decided to work at doing something worth-while for people. Do you know what I think?"

"Do you know how little I care what you think?"

Opal glanced at the rocks well beyond Daisy just to make sure. "I think," she said, still speaking gently, "that we're being spied upon, Maverick."

The girl gaped. The girl whirled King around and charged the distant rocks. She of course stopped charging when a carbine was brought up by a skinny bearded cuss who came around the rocks to meet her.

"Sir," Opal called, "you're the most beautiful fellow I've seen in years. If I didn't have a hero at home, I'd kiss you."

It was interesting to watch a cornered Prather in action. Maverick tensed as if to risk all on one mighty leap forward by King. Yet she was thinking, thinking, thinking all the time. She suddenly laughed so beautifully, so melodiously, the hair all but rose on Opal's scalp. "Mister," Maverick pleaded, "*will* you catch this fool horse so we can ride down?"

The bearded fellow stepped around her and King in a surprisingly businesslike way. He said to Maverick: "Git."

"Mister, you giving *me* orders?"

The carbine was fired.

She continued to think. She had to overcome this fellow or she had to do something or say something to retrieve the situation in another way.

So Maverick turned around, smiling. "You know," she said, "I believe this trash honestly thinks I was gonna leave you up here. For what reason? Anyone could walk down to the ranch."

"Folks coming," the bearded fellow told Opal. "Fast ridin', huh?"

Far below and across the range, there were indeed two riders coming along pell mell, heading for the Badlands. Maverick cried out furiously, "What's Tate doing here? What right has he to trespass on our range?"

And of course she panicked, Prather or not, just as an average scoundrel might in the circumstances. "My word against yours," she told Opal.

Opal nodded at the bearded man.

"Who listens to trash?" Maverick demanded. "All right, I was foolish. I made a mistake. I wanted to get even. How much will it cost me?"

Opal nodded again at the bearded man. He smiled. "Could use grub, could use lots of things."

"A job?" Opal prompted.

And the riders came closer, hitting the fringe of the Bandlands and slowing down somewhat, but not very much.

"Not with them," the bearded man told Opal. "One way or another, they cheat you. They loan you money, then squeeze you out."

And anyway, Opal thought, it wouldn't work out for a number of reasons, the chief one being that help blackmailed out of Maverick wouldn't be real help.

"Little lady," she said, "scat. No charge. From me to you, with love. But let me tell you something. You give yourself airs. You're nothing, really, that your father's money hasn't made you. You ride a horse you didn't earn, you wear clothes you didn't earn, you eat food you didn't earn. On your own, you're nothing. In fact, you're quite stupid. Now did you honestly believe I'd come here with the likes of you without a howitzer or two?"

It was quite enough, particularly when she

reached into the back pocket of her riding breeches and pulled out a derringer. "News for you," she said. "I may not be able to ride, but I really can shoot, courtesy of a war hero named Bert. Bert was shocked when he learned there was a Texan on earth who couldn't shoot."

Opal squeezed the trigger.

Maverick's Stetson went flying.

Ashen, speechless, Maverick went flying a half-second later, while the bearded fellow whooped laughter and slapped his thigh. "Girl," the bearded fellow said, "where you learn to shoot like that?"

But he scuttled, too, naturally, when the riders, Mike and Tate, came up at last.

Tate said, as only he could say: "Opal, art *is* long and time is indeed fleeting. I'm quite willing to humor you. I owe you much. However—"

Mike asked: "Okay, Opal?"

Opal got up from the rock and shoved the derringer back into her hip pocket. "Just lovely, Mike, just lovely. You don't much resemble the Confederate cavalry, however. Fancy meeting you here!"

He got down from his mount and stretched his legs. "What's her hurry about?" he asked, pointing. "Now, look, please don't say I'd drive any woman away in terror. I've heard that before. And please don't say she's hurrying down there to prepare our pre-wedding chow."

"No, just a contract, I suspect, giving me all the Prather publicity to handle. What with Bert and Tate and the Prathers, won't I be a busy girl?"

Tate said darkly: "My opinion on that arrangement, Opal, is subject to change at any moment."

Mike laughed. He ha-ha-ha-ed all over the place and finally took the rock she'd vacated. "What's money?" he asked. "The Prather girl has money, but what else?"

Tate looked at Opal, and then, very moodily, rode off down the trail. In the quiet you could hear the horse and the creaking saddle a long time.

"Funny thing about him," Mike finally said.

"If you shake him up a bit, he's okay. I went to his place to scoop you up and take you to Mexico. It's all a lot of propaganga written by women, this marriage stuff, but I figured that if that was what you wanted, I'd humor you. Well, when he told me you'd come up here with Maverick, I guess I went loco. That's how propaganda works, you know. If you read that mushstuff long enough, you get to believing some of it. And Tate, to give him his due, put the paintings and the music and the books away and came over here with me."

"Tate's a very nice fellow, Mike. Give me time and I'd marry him. We're at the brothersister stage now. Nice of you to decide to humor me."

"Ah, why not? I've slipped, Opal. There it is, on the line. I have in my office two beautiful women who think I'm all right to work for. Call it a career. Burn the black book, wear the beard and the carpet slippers, buy a house, drink beer and develop a paunch."

"How exciting for the girl, Mike!"

But she went to him and nudged him a bit and joined him on that rock. Knowing him better than he thought, she continued to ignore the naked fear deep in his lustrous black eyes. "But maybe," she said, "I've had enough excitement for a while. You mustn't ever be afraid for me, Mike. I mean that. I don't know all the answers to all the questions implicit in life. Who does, except God? But I do know that I'm adequate to meet many of the problems, particularly those posed by a badly spoiled girl, or a greedy Mr. Agnew, or a worried Mr. Prather, or even by a vain popinjay and flirt named Mike Lane."

"Hey," Mike snapped, "hey!"

Opal gazed out and away at the lowering sky and the vast land. "It's all mine, Mike, did you know? All the prizes. Down there, the Prathers are now in a dither, no doubt trying to figure out a graceful way to make me rich and still my tongue. I'll give them advice on the subject at the proper time . . . you know how we publicists are, always hatching an idea a second. And Bert Nutting is in the fold, so that puts the pressure on Mr. Agnew. You can't withstand that pressure, Mike, so you'll have to drop him, and then I'll add him to the fold. So will be born an agency, full-blown and enormously successful from the very beginning. And do you know why, Mike?"

Mike said tragically: "I'm bleeding."

"Because men can't handle life as women can, Mike. With men, it's one thing at a time. It's love or business or sports or something, one thing at a time. But a woman, being much the superior creature, being the center of life, indeed, can sit quite comfortably in the middle of confusion and keep her eye on all that matters and bring confusion to an end in a way beneficial to her. Or put it this way, Mike. A woman knows there must be a bean in the pot if love is to flower and bear rich fruit. Mike?"

He met her large blue eyes. "Well?"

"I have a bean, Mike."

He shrugged. A wind came across the great state of Texas and ruffled his coal-black hair. It was a rain wind. You could smell the moisture; you could see the long dry season coming to an end in the distance.

"Had enough?" Opal asked.

"Listen, I never did dump you! Will you get that through your noggin? Darn it, ask Ann! Ask at the bank! Every week—every week, get that—your check went to the bank. But business has to be business."

"Had enough?"

He scowled and wriggled and flushed and looked at the fingers of rain spearing the land in the distance. "We'll be drowned pretty soon," he said. "You coming or sitting here?"

"Coming where?"

"To Mexico. I'll give you a break. Take it or leave it. I'll snap my fingers and whistle once. If you don't come, that's it."

He climbed his horse awkwardly. He actually did snap his fingers and whistle, and Opal wanted to clout him.

Smiling, her heart drumming, Opal studied the sky and waited. She was kind when poor Mike dismounted, and graciously lured him back with a smile.